You Touched Me!

A Romantic Comedy in Three Acts

by Tennessee Williams and Donald Windham

Suggested by a short story of the same name by D.H. Lawrence

A SAMUEL FRENCH ACTING EDITION

SAMUEL FRENCH

FOUNDED 1830

New York Hollywood London Toronto

SAMUELFRENCH.COM

Copy of program of the first performance of *"You Touched Me!"* as produced at the Booth Theatre, New York City, September 26, 1945.

Guthrie McClintic

(In association with Lee Shubert)

presents

YOU TOUCHED ME!

A ROMANTIC COMEDY BY

TENNESSEE WILLIAMS and DONALD WINDHAM

SUGGESTED BY A SHORT STORY OF THE SAME NAME BY

D. H. LAWRENCE

STAGED BY MR. MC CLINTIC   SETTING BY MOTLEY

CAST

(In the order of their appearance)

MATILDA ROCKLEY.................*Marianne Stewart*

EMMIE ROCKLEY....................*Catherine Willard*

PHOEBE...........................*Norah Howard*

HADRIAN..........................*Montgomery Clift*

CORNELIUS ROCKLEY.................*Edmund Gwenn*

THE REVEREND GUILDFORD MELTON........*Neil Fitzgerald*

A POLICEMAN......................*Freeman Hammond*

The action takes place in a house in
rural England in the Spring of today.

ACT ONE

ACT ONE

Scene I

*The action takes place in a house in rural England in the
Spring of today.*
*It is the residence on the grounds of a pottery plant which
has been shut down since the beginning of the war.*
*There is one set, a cross section of the downstairs, which
consists of the living room on the Right and* CAPTAIN
ROCKLEY'S *cabin on the Left. In the Right wall are bayed
French doors leading into the garden. Right of Center at
the back is a hall which leads off Right to the kitchen. In
the Center at back are stairs leading to the upper part of
the house and to the front door in the Center of the back
wall. On the stair balcony is the door to* MATILDA'S *room
and a hallway beyond it. At Left of the landing is the door
to the cabin. There is a window in the Left wall of the
cabin.*
*Down Right in the living room is a what-not filled with
ornaments. In front of the French doors is a tea table with
chairs above, below and Right of it. A wall what-not with
a mirror is up Right; a spinet with stool near the back wall
Right Center; an end table and a deer's head which serves
as a hat rack, an umbrella stand under the rack are in the
kitchen hall. An end table Left of the stairs; a hat rack Left
of the front door.*
*An armchair Right Center; a sofa Center with desk and
chair back of it and a coffee-table in front of it; an arm
chair Left Center; and a bench in front of cabin platform
at Left in the living room.*

3

Inside the cabin there are stools up Right and down Left. A bunk with a port hole above it in the back wall. There is a shelf with ornaments above the bunk; a table Center with chairs Right and Left of it; a ship's wheel Left.

An important distinction must be made between this atmosphere and the sort of lightless heaviness and gloom that are associated, for example, with sets for the heavier dramas of Ibsen. As this is a lyrical comedy, it is essential that the stage should have an atmospheric charm. A clinging antiquity, a withdrawn quality must be expressed in a way that will show why those things were attractive to a timid girl like MATILDA. *The house has grace and beauty as many things do which nevertheless are not in vital contact with the world. As* MATILDA *observes at one point, the light through the vines that cover the windows "give such a cool, green color—like being under water." It is this dreamy, aqueous effect which should be realized—not heaviness or gloom!—Feminine ornaments, a multitude of them, are on shelves, and the colors of the room are gentle and pleasing. Hardly a sound comes in from the world outside, except when a locomotive arrives at the railroad station across the road, or when services are in progress at the church on the adjoining property. The war itself has not touched the house —it has hardly touched the village, for this is a town in a part of England that enemy bombers have overlooked.*

CAPTAIN CORNELIUS ROCKLEY *was once a sailor and the cabin reflects this. It is arranged to look as much like his cabin on his last command, the Polar Star, as can be managed in a small room in an old-fashioned house. It contains relics of voyages. The room is usually lighted by a hurricane lamp in a chimney of ruby glass. These things evoke the memory of a freer existence than the gentility of the rest of the house.*

Before the full stage lights come up, a pin spot of light ap-

pears on a large piece of heavy silver and the hands of
MATILDA *moving dreamily over its surface with a polishing
cloth. The light blooms gradually from this.* MATILDA *is at
the tea table, polishing silver and washing little glass ornaments. She is a girl of twenty and has the delicate, almost
transparent quality of glass. She might have stepped out of
a lyric by Shakespeare or Cowper or Spenser. Her dress is
pale yellow—she wears a dainty white apron and her hair
is tied up on her head with a white ribbon. The brilliant
metal has had an hypnotic effect on her. Her motions have
slowed to a halt.*

AUNT EMMIE *is a woman of forty with the feverish drive
that is characteristic of certain spinsters. She is not forbid-
ding. It is not* EMMIE *herself so much as the things she represents that are menacing—it is a characterization with
diverse aspects, which must be balanced as nicely, for in-
stance, as the laughable and appalling traits in Sidney
Howard's portrait of the mother in* The Silver Cord, *although what* EMMIE *represents is not predatory maternity
but aggressive sterility. She is at the mirror up Right.*

EMMIE. The fox was at it again last night. Mr. Melton says
the Wilkinsons were paid a call. Their chickens have been—
decimated! Oh, that fox!—nothing stops him! Barbed-
wire, fox-hounds, traps, poisons—nothing! But just let him
call on us— I'll give him a hot reception. [EMMIE *turns from
the mirror and sees* MATILDA *continuing the polishing in the
same dreamy fashion.*] Matilda, you were polishing that
same piece of silver when I left the house for the market.
[MATILDA'S *attention has turned inward again.*] Matilda!

MATILDA. [*Starting.*] I beg your pardon, Aunt Emmie.
What did you say?

EMMIE. I have to say everything twice. You drift out of
consciousness.

MATILDA. Whenever I look at anything awfully bright it makes me sleepy.

[*Barking outside.*]

EMMIE. Phoebe!

PHOEBE. [*Off in kitchen.*] Yes ma'am.

EMMIE. —Flora's attacking the postman! [PHOEBE, *the maid, scurries through from the kitchen to the front door. She is a buxom girl with nymph-like movements. Whenever she passes through,* EMMIE *stops short to regard her with suspicion. She is unable to decide whether the girl is simply sub-normal or actually subversive. As* PHOEBE *leaves.*] Embarrassing! [*To* MATILDA.] Sit up straight, don't hunch!

MATILDA. My shoulders are tired.

EMMIE. There is nothing more fatiguing than incorrect posture.

MATILDA. [*With tired humor.*] Perhaps some kind of tablets would help me.

EMMIE. Less dreaming would help you. I want you to be very bright this afternoon for Reverend Mr. Melton. He said to me after choir practice, "Your niece is very quiet." I said, "Oh, no, you should hear her about the house."

MATILDA. Aren't I fairly quiet about the house?

EMMIE. I didn't want him to think you have lock-jaw. This afternoon I want you to take some part in the conversation.

MATILDA. I think you can entertain him without my help.

EMMIE. Then you intend to give none?

MATILDA. But I was just wondering—wouldn't you like to be left alone for a while this afternoon with Mr. Melton?

EMMIE. I think those things have a way of arranging themselves. If you do leave us alone, don't do it ostentatiously.

MATILDA. You don't suppose he has taken the vow of celibacy, do you?

EMMIE. [*Alarmed at the suggestion.*] Heavens, no! What a notion! Whatever gave you that notion?

MATILDA. Oh, something about his manner. He's very high church, you know.

EMMIE. Not all *that* high church. My only concern is that he may learn of your father.

MATILDA. Father's drinking?—But don't you suppose he must have learned by now, having been in the parish two months?

EMMIE. Your father's been fairly good the past two months. I live in dread, however.

[*Shrill giggling heard out the front door.*]

PHOEBE. [*Off stage.*] How you go on.

EMMIE. [*Calling indignantly.*] Phoebe! Let the mail man go and bring in the mail. [*The door bangs open and* PHOEBE *trips in like a nymph pursued. She enters, unwrapping a small package.*] What have you there?

PHOEBE. [*Gurgling with surprise.*] A little birthday remembrance I got in the mail!

MATILDA. What is it, Phoebe?

PHOEBE. [*Holding them up.*] A pair of butterfly garters!

EMMIE. Pick up that tissue-paper.

PHOEBE. Ow, yiss.

EMMIE. Have *we* no mail?

PHOEBE. A *wire!* [*Hands it to* EMMIE. *Goes out to kitchen.*]

EMMIE. Do you suppose—[*She opens the wire.*]—that Cousin Aida has passed away finally?

[*The contents have a profoundly shocking effect—she sinks weakly on the sofa.*]

MATILDA. *Has* she?

EMMIE. If it was merely *that*, I wouldn't be knocked off my *feet.*

MATILDA. What is it, then?

EMMIE. [*As though she were pronouncing some loathsome disease.*] Your father's—*charity boy!*

MATILDA. Hadrian? [*She looks very startled.*]

EMMIE. This explains why your father has acted so foxy since he received that mysterious letter a few days ago. Hadrian is in England.

MATILDA. Is he discharged from the air force?

EMMIE. Doesn't say—just says— [*Reading from wire.*] "Expect me tomorrow. Flight Lieutenant Hadrian Rockley." Flight *Lieutenant* Hadrian Rockley! Flight Lieutenant Rockley, *if* you please! This was certainly not a gentleman's war! [*She makes a decisive gesture.*] *Well!* I have a bucket of water, *ice*-water, already filled to meet the situation. We'll deliberately omit all references to the war from our conversation.

MATILDA. [*With peculiar nervousness.*] I won't stay. I can't stay. I'll take a trip somewhere.

EMMIE. Because he's coming?

MATILDA. Yes.

EMMIE. I didn't know you disliked him as much as all that.

MATILDA. I don't dislike him at all.

EMMIE. Then why are you running away?

MATILDA. Nobody, nothing, has ever disturbed me so much as that boy did, living with us.

EMMIE. He was a thorn in my flesh.

MATILDA. Your feelings about him were not at all like mine. You weren't afraid of him.

EMMIE. Certainly not! Were you?

MATILDA. I felt unbearably self-conscious with him around. I couldn't speak to him in a natural voice.

EMMIE. Matilda!

MATILDA. I don't know why. I would even cry sometimes, because I could feel how lonely the boy must be. He was very neat and clean and nice in his appearance.

EMMIE. He used to spit on his shoes to shine them—ugh!—like an alley-cat!

MATILDA. That's how you treated him—like an alley-cat. And he always treated you with such respect.

EMMIE. [Grinning.] Like one of those excessively friendly clerks who've just given you half an ounce short measure.

MATILDA. Are you going to be rude to him?

EMMIE. Being a well-bred person, I'm going to treat him politely.

MATILDA. Nicely politely or nastily politely?

EMMIE. With dignity! To keep him in his place! And encourage his prompt return to the Dominion of Canada.

[*There is a disturbance outside in the garden.* PHOEBE *bounces in from the kitchen.*]

PHOEBE. Miss Emmie, Oh, Miss Emmie! A collier's dog got through the 'edge. He wants to know if he can come in and get it.

EMMIE. [*Crossing to the French doors.*] He'll get it from me if he steps foot in the garden. [*Sighting him in the yard.*] Oh, my goodness, he's planted his oafish feet right smack in our petunias! [*Marching out at him.*] *You! Collier!*

MATILDA. [*To* PHOEBE.] Lieutenant Hadrian Rockley is coming tomorrow.

PHOEBE. A relation, Miss?

MATILDA. Yes, in a way, he is. An adopted relation.

PHOEBE. [*Pleased.*] He'd be a young officer, now?

MATILDA. A young officer? Yes.

PHOEBE. [*Beaming.*] How nice—to have a young officer here!

EMMIE. [*Enters from garden, carrying Flora.*] His dog got the worst of it—much! He scudded back through the hedge like he'd seen a Chinese devil.

MATILDA. Good for Flora!

EMMIE. Phoebe, take Flora away. [PHOEBE *complies and goes into the kitchen.*] I think that's the collier that delivers the rum to your father. Oh, Matilda, supposing he'd made a delivery just now. Wouldn't that be the wickedness of fate to have the Captain go on a drunk this very afternoon? Oh, Oh, Oh! If I thought that would happen with Mr. Melton coming for tea.

[*A burst of raucous singing arises from the rear of the house. The sound appears to have a petrifying effect upon the two* WOMEN. *They stop short and exchange a horrified stare. The song is not in English. It is one of those loud disonant Oriental tunes* CAPTAIN ROCKLEY *picked up in his youth as a sailor. Phoenetically spelled out, it sounds like this:*]

CAPTAIN. O Takhi Sahn, O mi won aye,
        Boom! Bong!

EMMIE. [*Hoarsely.*] *Your father!*

CAPTAIN. O Takhi Sahn, O mahbah bows,
        BOOM! BONG!
        Eeeeeee——Owwwwwwww!
        Takhi, Takhi, Takhi, Takhi,
        S-a-a-a-an!
        BOOM! BONG!

MATILDA. [*Gravely nodding.*] O Takhi Sahn!! [EMMIE *sinks helplessly on the sofa, clasping her forehead.*] Now, Aunt Emmie, don't go to pieces.

EMMIE. Ah, that infernal collier. It was he that delivered the bottles.

MATILDA. Father couldn't have drunk enough to sing "O Takhi Sahn" already, if it was the collier.

EMMIE. Then he is anticipating. I have known him to finish a pint at one swallow. I noticed him in the garden when I went out—he probably has the bottle concealed on the grounds. Matilda, I despair. Despair completely!

MATILDA. *Don't!* I think we can sober him up before tea time.

EMMIE. Our only chance is to find where he has hidden the bottle. I'll watch out the window in case he sneaks back out. You keep an eye in here. *Ahh! There he goes.* He's slipping around in back of the pottery shed. [*Crosses to French doors.*] I'm going to nip this spree in the bud. [*She rushes out.*]

[MATILDA *with sorrowful shake of the head, goes back to polishing the silver and in a few moments she is staring dreamily into space under the hypnotic spell of the brilliant metal. Her movements slow to a halt. There is the sound of a train pulling in and the clanging of iron bells. After a little while, the front door is pushed open and* HADRIAN *enters quietly. At this moment the sun emerges. The smoke from the engine which is directly across the road puffs into the open door about his figure and the mist has a yellowish glow.* HADRIAN *is a clean-cut, muscular young man in the dress uniform of a lieutenant in the Royal Canadian Air Force. There is something about him which the unsympathetic might call sharp or fox-like. It is a look, certainly, that might be observed in the face of a young animal of the woods who has preserved his life through tense exercise of a physical craft and quickness; an alert, inquisitive look. To avoid a complication in casting the part, we will not say that he has red hair, but hair of that color would suit his kind of vital, quick awareness. Behind that quickness is something else— a need, a sensitivity, a sad patient waiting for something. That something else comes out in his face as he enters the door and stands for a moment looking intently at* MATILDA'S *turned back and self-absorbed stillness. After a moment it turns to a grin. He puts his cap on the desk. He advances softly, stealing up behind her and setting down his valise.*

MATILDA *is so unaware that she does not notice him until he speaks.*]

HADRIAN. [*Gently.*] *Our Matilda!*

MATILDA. [*Turns with a gasp, a silver card tray clattering to the floor.*] Hadrian!

HADRIAN. [*Still grinning, but awkward.*] You—seem surprised.

MATILDA. I—am.

HADRIAN. Didn't you get my wire?

MATILDA. It said tomorrow.

HADRIAN. Commando raid! I didn't want you to go to a lot of fuss. [*He picks up the dropped card tray and hands it to her. She holds it before her, as if she were expecting him to place something on it.*] What are you planning to do—put out my eyes with all of that fine silver?

MATILDA. Yes—I mean—we didn't want you to find us looking like this.

HADRIAN. So I've caught you off guard. That's good! [*He laughs and starts to kiss her, but she straightens shyly and extends her hand. He keeps hold of it until she nervously pulls it away.*] How are you, Matilda?

MATILDA. Oh, I'm—pretty well. [*She continues to look at him unbelievingly.*] You've *changed.*

HADRIAN. Sure I have. I've done all kinds of things to make me change. I went out to Canada, you know.

MATILDA. Yes.

HADRIAN. Worked in a light and power plant in Montreal.

MATILDA. You seem as though you had.

HADRIAN. Then when the war broke out, I took to the air.

MATILDA. Father has made a scrap-book of your letters.

HADRIAN. Did you read them?

MATILDA. They were read aloud. The Captain reads them to us over and over.

HADRIAN. The *Captain*, by God! Where *is* he?

MATILDA. Outside, right now.

HADRIAN. Aunt Emmie?

MATILDA. She's outside, too.

HADRIAN. I'll *find* them!—I know where he is.—I'll get him in—he's in the pot shed.

MATILDA. No, *please*, it's better you wait till they come back in. Won't you sit down?

HADRIAN. [*Laughs and sits down awkwardly. It seems difficult for him to remain still.*] I've been making a lot of noise, haven't I?

MATILDA. [*Laughing breathlessly.*] Yes, you have—a bit.

HADRIAN. Do you mind if I look around a bit?

MATILDA. Of course not.

HADRIAN. [*Rising.*] The cabin! The cabin! [*He opens the cabin door and turns on the hurricane lamp. He looks almost reverently around the room which is the only place he ever felt really at home.*] Of the Polar Star—

MATILDA. It hasn't changed.

HADRIAN. Oh, no, oh, no—some things, I guess, *don't*

change. [*As soon as he is out of sight,* MATILDA *touches her forehead and closes her eyes. Her perturbation is only understandable to the shy, for whom all intimacy is rich with danger.* HADRIAN *comes to the table and picks up a flute.*] Hey! Guess what I have found?—[*Comes back to the living room.*]

MATILDA. I don't know.—What is it?

HADRIAN. [*Laughing.*] My penny flute. Do you remember my penny flute, Matilda?

MATILDA. Oh, yes, we've kept it for you.

HADRIAN. Imagine that! [*Laughs incredulously.*]—so long!

MATILDA. Only—well—five years . . .

HADRIAN. [*Looking about with slow wonder.*] *Hey!*

MATILDA. What?

HADRIAN. This can't be true! No change! No change at all!

MATILDA. You expected some changes?

HADRIAN. [*First uncertainly: then quite definitely.*]—Yes —*Yes!*

MATILDA. There were changes during the war, but now everything's slipping back to normal again.

HADRIAN. Just as it was, you mean, as if nothing had happened? The pottery plant is going to resume operations? Going to go on making little round, empty bowls, now that the little fuss in the Yard's blown over? [MATILDA *looks at him with surprise which is somewhat fearful.*] Excuse me— I'm shouting again, I had forgotten how out of place a loud voice is in here. You'll have to watch me.

MATILDA. It won't be necessary.

HADRIAN. I want to make a go of it with Emmie.

MATILDA. I'm afraid you are going to find it a rather dull place for a flier to return to.

HADRIAN. No, but—how do you find it?

MATILDA. Oh, that's quite different—I've never lived anywhere else. Just now, just lately—I've been invited to London by Cousin Aida.

HADRIAN. Going, are you?—*When?*

MATILDA. [*Inventing hastily.*] Tonight. Tonight or—tomorrow.

HADRIAN. Put it off for a while.

MATILDA. I'm not sure I can. I've dental work to be done and—

HADRIAN. It wasn't nice of me to just bust in.

MATILDA. We only got your wire a minute ago. I wasn't prepared to see you and— Well, you left a boy, now you've come back grown up—changed into a man.

HADRIAN. Well, you've grown into a woman.

MATILDA. [*Obscurely embarrassed by this observation.*] You'll excuse me if I go on with the silver.

HADRIAN. Sure. Go right ahead.

MATILDA. Aunt Emmie's having a tea this afternoon for the new rector, the Reverend Mr. Melton.

HADRIAN. I've come at just the wrong moment.

MATILDA. You've no such thing. Aunt Emmie will be *so*

pleased that you did come for it. She was just saying what a pity it was you'd have to miss it.

HADRIAN. Has she forgiven me, then?

MATILDA. For what?

HADRIAN. For my five years' intrusion.

MATILDA. What a thing to call it. [HADRIAN *blows softly on the penny flute.*] I'm afraid we never made you feel at home. It was all a muddle of misunderstandings.

HADRIAN. [*Continues staring at her.*] Do you realize you and I let down the bars only once.

MATILDA. What do you mean?

HADRIAN. That time the storm broke on the way home from school—and there was a big crash of thunder—you grabbed my arm. [*He catches his arm.*]

MATILDA. I was afraid of storms.

HADRIAN. You were afraid of everything in those days.

MATILDA. I still am.

HADRIAN. We looked at each other and laughed and started talking as if we'd just then met—instead of having lived under the same roof for—how long was it?—Five years! [*This recollection embarrasses* MATILDA. *She polishes the silver tray very rapidly.*] You're going to polish right through that piece of silver.

MATILDA. [*Laughs nervously and puts it aside.*] Oh!

HADRIAN. It never happened again, that friendly meeting. So I gave up and left.

MATILDA. Ever since we heard you'd gone in the Air Force, I've mentioned your name at every Holy Communion.

HADRIAN. [*Stares at her a moment, then laughs gently.*] Matilda, you're so—out of the world.—On nights that I've bombed Berlin you've played the piano. You've polished silver while I've blown up cities. I bet you don't know there was a war going on—on the other side of the privet hedge.

MATILDA. Oh, yes—we were bombed once.

HADRIAN. No!

MATILDA. Just before one Christmas, a bomb fell a block away. The vibration broke two windows in the house.

HADRIAN. Two windows!

MATILDA. And sixteen bowls were cracked in the pottery sheds.

HADRIAN. But still you've carried on. What makes the grounds so quiet? The vines have grown over the windows!

MATILDA. Yes, they have.

HADRIAN. Doesn't anyone trim them?

MATILDA. We prefer them like that. They give such a cool, green color, like being under water.

HADRIAN. How about boy friends—Matilda?

MATILDA. What?

HADRIAN. Fellows you have dates with! Don't tell me you haven't a soldier boy sweetheart, Matilda.

MATILDA. I can't say I have. [*A little sharply.*] I've been trying to tell you, nothing has changed one bit in the pottery house.

HADRIAN. And you? What have you been doing?

MATILDA. [*Very hesitantly.*] I—well—I've written *these!*

[*She produces a scrap book from under the table.*]

HADRIAN. [*Opening it.*] Poems!

MATILDA. [*With embarrassed pride.*] They're clipped from various papers that printed them.

HADRIAN. [*Reading at random.*] "How like a caravan my heart— Across the desert moved toward yours!" [*Looks up, grinning.*] Toward whose? Who is this H.C. it's dedicated to?

MATILDA. [*Again takes the silver tray and polishes it rapidly.*] Hart Crane. An American poet who died ten years ago.

HADRIAN. Well, that's all right. A perfectly safe romance.

PHOEBE. [*Rushing in from the kitchen.*] Miss Matilda! Miss Emmie's located the bottle. They're *wrestling* for it.

MATILDA. I'll have to go out.

HADRIAN. Shall *I* go?

MATILDA. No, no! You'd better not. Don't let him know you've caught him in this condition. We were so hoping he'd try to be nice and sober for your home-coming.

HADRIAN. What shall I do? Shall I hide?

MATILDA. Yes!

HADRIAN. Where? Under the spinet. [*Slips behind spinet.*]

MATILDA. Till we get him upstairs. Then we'll tell him you're coming and maybe he'll straighten out. Phoebe, draw him a bath and make black coffee! [*She starts out French doors.*]

HADRIAN. Hey! Wait! My cap! That would give me away.

[*Coming to desk, he takes his cap and returns back of spinet.*]

PHOEBE. [*Gapes at* HADRIAN.] Why, you must be—

HADRIAN. Shhhh!

[*He grins at the sound of the altercation which is growing louder and more violent.* CAPTAIN ROCKLEY *enters from the garden, followed by* EMMIE, *dishevelled and completely distracted, anything but the stately figure that she would present to the world.* CAPTAIN ROCKLEY *is a pretty shocking spectacle. He has a bellowing voice, there is something epic in his frustrated fury and outrageousness. He wears a peacoat over his undershirt and has on a pair of ancient dungarees, a battered cap on the back of his head.*]

EMMIE. Either you give up that bottle, or I shall phone for the doctor to send that male nurse around with the straitjacket.

CAPTAIN. Threats, threats! Wasted breath! Change is coming.

EMMIE. For you, it is. The mad house!

CAPTAIN. That old threat doesn't intimidate me. I'm not to be kept in permanent subjection. I've still got violence in me. Just because the Polar Star piled up and they took away my papers—that don't mean I belong with—tabby-cats. [*Crouching and glaring into her face.*] *Tabby*-cats! [*Very craftily.*] I know something you *don't*, Sister Emmie.

EMMIE. Don't be so sure about that!

CAPTAIN. [*Bellowing.*] Hadrian's coming!

EMMIE. You thought you'd spring him again by surprise? *I* know he's coming.

CAPTAIN. And so I'll have protection! [*He makes a lumbering dash for the stairs.*]

EMMIE. Indeed! If your snivelling little charity boy interferes, I'll turn him out so fast it will make his head swim.

CAPTAIN. Oh, no you won't; we'll see about that.

MATILDA. [*She is horribly shocked by the knowledge that* HADRIAN *has overheard.*] Oh, Aunt Emmie!

[AUNT EMMIE *has started for the stairs, continuing her pursuit of the* CAPTAIN. *A sound arrests her. It is the penny flute. The* CAPTAIN *has reached the landing—he stops, too. The light but plaintive air comes from back of the spinet. For a moment* EMMIE *stares at it dumbly. Slowly over the top of the spinet, appears the cap and the head.* EMMIE *catches her breath. All she can do is stare. From the stairs the* CAPTAIN *cannot see* HADRIAN. *He lumbers grotesquely down. When he catches sight of the boy, he utters a shout of laughter that is almost crying.*]

CAPTAIN. Hadrian! [HADRIAN *removes the flute from his lips and grins—the awkward charity boy.*] Hadrian! [HADRIAN *steps from behind the spinet. The* CAPTAIN *advances toward him unsteadily, both arms extended.*] God Almighty! Back to the Polar Star! [*Embraces him. Over* HADRIAN'S *shoulder, to* EMMIE *and* MATILDA *who remain motionless.*] Now, you women—see! The sides are even.

CURTAIN

ACT ONE

Scene II

A few hours later. Tea has been served in the garden and it is now toward sunset. The interior of the-house is cool and dim, but through the doors to the garden a misty gold light is admitted.

MATILDA *is standing up Right near the mirror, having just hurried in from the garden. She is elegantly dressed and looks very pretty and quite remote. She has on a soft pearl grey chiffon dress with a string of green crystal beads. She is staring at herself in the mirror as* EMMIE *rushes in from the garden.*

EMMIE. Matilda! It's impossible to stay in the garden any longer. It's getting so cold out there we're turning blue. We shall have to come inside. Now, you—the first convenient moment go upstairs and help Phoebe stand guard over the Captain. I'm in mortal dread he'll get past her. I haven't drawn one free breath and the pressure of gas on my heart is really alarming. Ouuuu! Palpitations!

MATILDA. Drink hot soda water.

EMMIE. And belch?—Why did you drift away and leave me single-handed?

MATILDA. I thought I would lose my mind.

EMMIE. Hadrian?

MATILDA. He stares at me so.

EMMIE. Boorish!

MATILDA. I didn't know where to look. I had to get up and come in.

EMMIE. Brazen, graceless!

MATILDA. Now that he's opened up some, why, he shows a very bright and manly sort of character.

EMMIE. Mannie, detestably mannie!

HADRIAN. [*Enters from garden to hear this last observation.*] Are you criticizing the little minister?

EMMIE. Have you left him alone?

HADRIAN. No. I came to fetch my tobacco. Why did *you* run away, Matilda?

EMMIE. You stared her out of countenance, that's why. [MATILDA *has moved nervously to the spinet.*]

HADRIAN. I was just admiring that soft, filmy stuff she's got on. I wanted to touch it.

EMMIE. [*Waspishly.*] We'll cut you off a piece to keep in your pocket.

HADRIAN. But she ought to wear brighter colors.

EMMIE. During the rest of Hadrian's visit, Matilda, you must keep yourself wrapped up in the Union Jack. Someone must go back out. This is very rude.

HADRIAN. The Captain's still hitting the ball pretty hard up there.

EMMIE. What? How do you know?

HADRIAN. He threw something out the window. A butterfly garter.

EMMIE. Phoebe's! Merciful Heavens! Was it noticed?

HADRIAN. Oh, yes—it landed in the minister's lap.

EMMIE. Matilda, go, go, go! I'm blind with panic. [MA-TILDA *crosses below her out to the garden.*] Hadrian, try to help us cover things up. [HADRIAN *crosses below her out to the garden.* EMMIE *standing Right end of the spinet.*] If anything dreadful happens I'm going to die!

CAPTAIN. [*From off upstairs.*] O Tahki Sahn! O My one Aye! O My *one Aye!* Boom! Bong!

[PHOEBE *yells; starts downstairs.* EMMIE *crosses to steps.*]

PHOEBE. No, no! Stop it, stop it, Mr. Rockley!

EMMIE. In the name of Heaven! What is going on?

PHOEBE. It's Mr. Rockley, Mum, 'e's ticklin' me!

[CAPTAIN *starts downstairs.* PHOEBE *yells.*]

CAPTAIN. Come back here, Phoebe. Give me my bottle.

[PHOEBE *goes into cabin. Closes door.*]

EMMIE. [*Up on landing.*] Cornelius Rockley!

CAPTAIN. She took my bottle.

EMMIE. [*Holding him; back to cabin door.*] Go back up-stairs. I'll see that she brings it to you. [*Calls to* PHOEBE.] For Heaven's sake, Phoebe, open the door and help get him *back upstairs.* [*Ad Lib off garden.*] No, no, it's too late! He'll have to stay here. [CAPTAIN *goes into cabin followed by* EMMIE.] Phoebe, don't dare let him out! *Cornelius,* if you come out, I will never forgive you, *never!*

[CAPTAIN *sits in chair Right.* EMMIE *comes out of the cabin —closes door.* PHOEBE *stands with back against cabin door.*]

REVEREND. [*Entering from the garden; crosses to Right Center. He carries a tea cup.*] Are you quite ready for us?

[*He is a rather mincing little man who lays great stress on refinement of voice and gesture. He and* EMMIE *both think he is very witty. He is the type that is heavily playful and only gets his own jokes.*]

EMMIE. Oh, yes, indeed, I was just— [*Crosses to back of desk.*]

REVEREND. It suddenly turned quite chilly in the garden.

EMMIE. Shade makes such a difference. I think we'd all better get into some wraps.

REVEREND. Oh, but we're not to be sent back out again, are we?

EMMIE. Sent? Mr. Melton, no! But the sunset simply has to be seen from the arbor.

MATILDA. [*Eagerly.*] We mustn't miss it.

REVEREND. Regrettable as missing it would be—my bronchial condition makes it unwise to stay out.

EMMIE. [*Aside to* MATILDA.] The Captain—downstairs— in the study!

REVEREND. I hoped to have the pleasure of meeting the senior Mr. Rockley this afternoon.

EMMIE. I hope you will excuse him today.

REVEREND. He's not at home?

EMMIE. Yes, but he's quite a scholar He's intensely absorbed at the moment in preparing an article.

REVEREND. An article! For what?

EMMIE. The—er—Royal Geographic Society.

REVEREND. Interesting! Extremely! On what subject?

EMMIE. [*Touching her forehead.*] Oh, yes—what *is* the subject, Matilda?

MATILDA. [*Faintly.*] I believe some thoughts on—navigation.

[*The* CAPTAIN *during this has been peeking out study door.* PHOEBE *tries to draw him back. The scuffle is audible.*]

EMMIE. The gardener's—putting up curtains. What a trial servants are these days! Matilda, ask them to be a little quieter.

[MATILDA *self-consciously withdraws to the cabin. With imploring pantomime she gets the* CAPTAIN *back from the door and sets up a checkerboard on the table for him during the following.*]

REVEREND. Here is something that fell from an upstairs window. [*He produces the butterfly garter from his pocket.*]

EMMIE. Why—what *is* it?

REVEREND. [*Urbanely.*] I judge it to be sŏme part of a lady's apparel.

EMMIE. Ah, that rascally dog—our little Pekinese—he throws things out! I wonder if you have heard that amusing story of how the Pekinese originated?

REVEREND. No. How did they originate?

EMMIE. [*Adjusting the curtains between the hall and the living room.*] A lion fell in love with a squirrel and said to Buddha, "Buddha, I have fallen in love with a squirrel. I would like to be the squirrel's size so we can be married, but I would like to keep the courage of the lion!" Buddha granted his prayer and created the Pekinese!

REVEREND. [*Thinking the story not finished.*] Yes?

EMMIE. [*Seeing that he has missed the point.*] That is—uh —how the Pekinese originated.

REVEREND. Oh? [*He suddenly gets it or supposes he should.*] Oh!—Originated!—Quite! [*He laughs politely.*]

[MATILDA *returns to the room.* HADRIAN *re-enters with tea cup.*]

EMMIE. Shall we—sit down? [*Sitting on the sofa.*]

REVEREND. Thank you. [*He looks about him vaguely.*]

EMMIE. [*Indicating chair Left of the sofa.*] Here you are, Mr. Melton.

REVEREND. Uh—thank you. [*He sits down carefully. There is an awkward pause.* EMMIE *clears her throat.*] An angel must be flying over the house.

HADRIAN. [*Politely.*] Why do you say that, Mr. Melton?

REVEREND. That's what it means when everybody is silent.

[*The* CAPTAIN *has taken a position at the cabin door to observe through a crack. He whistles softly between his teeth to catch* HADRIAN'S *attention who stands nearest the cabin. Fortunately* REVEREND MELTON'S *perceptions are not very quick and while certain untoward things now and then catch his attention he is never aware of their entire implication.* EMMIE, *however, is on pins and needles.* MATILDA *sits on sofa.*]

EMMIE. [*Quickly.*] We haven't discussed our plans for the meeting tonight.

REVEREND. Oh—uh—The Women's Athenaeum!

EMMIE. You *will* be there, Mr. Melton?

REVEREND. If I can get away from The Girls' Brigade!

EMMIE. We have such an interesting program for tonight. Matilda will read her valedictory poem to Virginia Woolf and *I*—well—*I've* prepared a paper.

REVEREND. Good for you! On what?

EMMIE. [*Rather grandly.*] A critical thesis. "Shaw, Lawrence, Wells, and other false Prophets of Pragmatism!"

[REVEREND *purrs approvingly.*]

HADRIAN. [*Leaning on the Right end of the spinet.*] Aunt Emmie, what is pragmatism?

EMMIE. I'm afraid the definition would only confuse you.

HADRIAN. [*Abruptly.*] Excuse me, but all this— [*He sets his tea cup down with a little bang.*]

EMMIE. [*Involuntarily.*] Careful of that tea cup! All this—what?

HADRIAN. [*Speaks with an excitement that is gradually tinged with violence as he comes down Right of sofa.*] Pragmatism and—tea and—Matilda's dress! I haven't tied in with it yet.

EMMIE. A mystifying remark! Will you explain it?

HADRIAN. Aw, it's just that I've come downstairs so lately. And upstairs—well—the atmosphere's more rugged. [*He grins engagingly but* EMMIE *is not mollified.*]

REVEREND. Up—stairs?

HADRIAN. The sky over Europe!

EMMIE. Hadrian, move away from that what-not shelf. You're going to forget yourself and lean against it, and while there is nothing particularly valuable on it, I'd just as soon not have them all smashed to pieces.

[*A whistle from study.* EMMIE *clears her throat.*]

HADRIAN. [*Placatingly.*] Don't get me wrong. [*He moves away a little from the shelf.*] I like all this—pragmatism and tea and—Matilda's dress! But—but—I can't tell you.

EMMIE. Hadrian! If you don't get away from that what-not shelf I'm going to remove it.—Now take a position somewhere and settle yourself, or if you're really too nervous then take a bromide.

HADRIAN. I have no nerves; and yet when I walked back into this place this morning my blood ran cold with amazement. I—I—I can't tell you.

EMMIE. Well, don't try, then.

HADRIAN. The trouble is that I've been a bomber pilot. I've bombed Berlin. And Hamburg and Bremen, Cologne and Ludwigshaven. [MATILDA *crosses to* REVEREND *and takes his tea cup.*] I've flown over cities and watched those cities blow up like boxes of matches. Then flown back over the channel, as calm as Matilda crosses to take a tea cup.

REVEREND. Thank you, Miss Matilda.

HADRIAN. But I'm not mechanical—all a machine.

EMMIE. Who ever said you were?

HADRIAN. I know what I've committed—atrocities!

REVEREND. I beg your pardon!

HADRIAN. Whoever does it, whatever reason you give—

it's still an atrocity when you blow up a city! And it leaves you feeling—maybe not guilty, but—somehow a little—*responsible* for—things! "Everything's slipped back to normal" says Matilda—and she smiles.—Excuse me, but I can't smile. Y'see "back to normal" was not quite all we dreamed of.

EMMIE. What did you dream of?

HADRIAN. Change!

REVEREND. [*Indulgently.*] "Change" is such a beautiful abstraction.

HADRIAN. [*Roughly.*] The hell with "abstraction."

EMMIE. Hadrian!

HADRIAN. Change can also be—*action!*—And *will* be, Mr. Melton. And *will* be, Emmie. Yes, it *will* be, Matilda. Don't you—believe me? Or are you convinced it's going to stay like it was except for there being the finest new bunch of ruins for tourists to visit since Pompeii.

REVEREND. [*Cautiously.*] What sort of "change" or "action" did you—envisage?

HADRIAN. The old frontiers! Frontiers of thinking—frontiers of the mind!

REVEREND. The—uh—mind?

HADRIAN. Yes. You've heard of it, surely.

EMMIE. Hadrian! Mr. Melton has studied at Oxford.

REVEREND. Youth, Miss Emmie! Youth! You spoke of pushing them out?

HADRIAN. By putting less faith in fences—more in the open range. Now the war's over—we've got to explore new countries of the mind, and colonize them. Not just a Columbus or two, but whole great boat-loads of fearless colonists have to set foot in those countries and make homes there—not prefabricated—but on a vast and everlasting-scale! And there mustn't be any peace, but a new war's beginning.

REVEREND. Another war?

EMMIE. Heaven forbid!

HADRIAN. The war for life, not against it. The war to create a world that can live without war. All the dead bodies of Europe, all of the corpses of Africa, Asia, America ought to be raised on flagpoles over the world, and the cities not built up but left as they are—a shambles, a black museum— for you and you and you—to stroll about in—on Sunday afternoons—in case you forget—and leave the world to chance, and the rats of advantage.

CAPTAIN. [*From behind cabin door.*] Hear! Hear!

REVEREND. A Daniel come to judgment!

HADRIAN. I didn't know that I had all that on my chest. I feel better. I suppose I've shocked you? Have I shocked you, Matilda?

MATILDA. No, you haven't shocked me. I was—impressed.

EMMIE. I think we were all impressed one way or another. You've certainly found your tongue. When you were here before you were like a closed book.

REVEREND. Well, now it is opened. You've made me wonder whether that decoration was given for fighting or *speaking*.

EMMIE. Mr. Melton is speaking to you, Hadrian.

HADRIAN. Is he? What did he say?

REVEREND. Nothing of the slightest importance.

EMMIE. I think the point was well taken. I shall give him a decoration, too. Hadrian I shall give you a fox's brush— provided you shoot the fox.

REVEREND. Ah, so you, too, have received a visit from the—

EMMIE. Not yet, but I am all ready to greet him— I have a loaded gun at the foot of the stairs and I'm not a bad shot. I can't stand foxes.

[*The* CAPTAIN *leaves off eavesdropping. He flops noisily on the bunk where* PHOEBE *has been relaxing. She springs up, squealing.*]

EMMIE. Matilda, how was your father getting along with his—article on navigation?

MATILDA. Oh, he's—describing a storm.

REVEREND. I once knew a writer who got so wrapped up in his subject he'd act out the parts while he wrote. Once while writing about a young man who jumped out of a tenth story window— Well—the book was never finished.

EMMIE. [*Laughing airily.*] Oh, Mr. Melton, you're so full of delightful stories. Hadrian, why don't you go and help Mr. Rockley get his ship around the—-Straits of Magellan?

HADRIAN. Sure. [*He crosses to cabin door.*]

EMMIE. After that violent talk, I think we might have some music to quiet our nerves.

REVEREND. Indeed we might.

EMMIE. You remember that we exacted your promise to sing.

REVEREND. Now, Miss Emmie!

EMMIE. What excuse can you offer?

REVEREND. Clergyman's throat!

EMMIE. It is not accepted. [*She draws him toward the spinet.*]

[*Lights down—up in cabin.* HADRIAN *enters the cabin. The* CAPTAIN *springs up to embrace him. The* REVEREND'S *vocal selection is muted as through a closed door. He has a fairly good tenor voice and the music should provide a pleasing background for the dialogue in the study.* EMMIE *or* MATILDA *might sing with him in the second chorus. A recording had better be used. "Oh, That We Two Were Maying!" would be a good number.*]

CAPTAIN. Hadrian, boy! A glorious speech you made, I heard you make it.

HADRIAN. [*Closing the door.*] Shhhh!

CAPTAIN. Don't shush me.

HADRIAN. You've got your sister sitting on pins and needles.

CAPTAIN. Good for 'er. [*Snatches up the penny flute from the table.*] Let's take our instrument an' join th' concert.

PHOEBE. [*Despairingly.*] Oh, Mr. 'Adrian!

HADRIAN. We're not wanted in there.

CAPTAIN. Phoebe, see this flute? I heard him blowin' it in the yard of an orphan's home in Chelsea. A sad little song—What was it?

HADRIAN. Danny Boy!

CAPTAIN. I stopped at th' fence he was perched on. I said to
him, "Son, are you afraid of wimmen?" "I don't know,
Sir," he answered, "I don't know any!" I got his release
from the charity institution an' brought him home to protect
me from my sister. Five years he did. Then quit me.—Left
me only the penny flute, you blighter! [*Hands flute to* HA-
DRIAN.]

HADRIAN. Now I've come back.

CAPTAIN. Against me?

HADRIAN. No, sir, with you!

CAPTAIN. You don't even know what the situation is. Look
at me. Pusillanimous! Held in restraint by women. My legs
're swollen—they say it's dropsy. Dropsy, hell—it's wimmen. I'm soft an' swollen up with the constant watch an'
touch an' care of wimmen. Ain't that so, Phoebe?

PHOEBE. Ow, yis, indeed, Mr. Rockley!

CAPTAIN. She ought to know—being one of the female
watchers! Look at 'er, look at 'er! What do you think of
that stuff? Why, I have seen more charm in a—female
porpoise!

PHOEBE. Huh!

CAPTAIN. Have you ever seen a female porpoise, boy?

HADRIAN. No, sir.

CAPTAIN. Not bad, not bad at all. [*His eyes gleam reminis-
cently as he pours* HADRIAN *a drink.*] The possibilities of
the female porpoise are not so limited as a man would suppose who hadn't had my unique experience with 'em. When
I was a boy—

PHOEBE. Ow, Mr. 'Adrian, please don't let 'im repeat that disgustin' story!

CAPTAIN. Pipe down—you—pipe dov·n! When I was a younger turkey-cock than you—I sailed one August out of Vera Cruz on a full-rigged ship that was called The Lady of Pearls. Hurricane struck her—the Lady went down off the coast of Nicaragua— For nineteen days I hung on a galley-hatch— Me and eternity and a—female porpoise— Yes, sir, I had a companion, a female porpoise—she swam around me so close I could have touched her— This female porpoise had fallen in love with me. I had grown a beard, a bright red beard—she liked it. Ev'ry few minutes she heaved up out of the drink an' cocked her eyes at me— *Sssstttt!*—she went—like that. [*Jerks his head to one side with a leer.*]

[HADRIAN *grins.*]

PHOEBE. [*Doubtfully sits in chair Left.*] Huh.

CAPTAIN. The first time she done it—"Well, damn your impudence." I shouted.—I spit in 'er eye. I was a little—fastidious in those days. A few minutes later—up she pops again—*Sssssstttt!*—like that. Only more—provocative than ever. "Madam," I says to the porpoise, "you're wastin' your time. It's out of the question, not only abominable but— not possible even!" In those days—well—a Protestant up-bringin'— [*Drinks.*] Discouraged 'er? Not a bit!—Up again—third time—*Sssttt!* [HADRIAN *blows an exclamatory note on the flute.* CAPTAIN *continues, benignly philosophical.*] Well, well, well—after all—proprieties—congruities— What are they?—all the little notions and niceties of our so-called—culturization! What are they in the eyes of the Everlastin'? Of God—or a female porpoise! *Nada!*— meaning *nothin'!* A red-bearded boy fifty miles off the coast of Nicaragua! Where was the stone? And who was likely to cast it?

HADRIAN. The fourth time?

CAPTAIN. *Sssssstttt!* [*Gestures and leers.*] By that time—well—I was makin'—observations! Among other things—.I observed that the female porpoise was not altogether a fish.

HADRIAN. A mermaid, was she?

CAPTAIN. A *mammal!*—God bless 'em. An' bein' a mammal she had a mammal's equipment! [*He curves his hands around imaginary protrusions.*]

HADRIAN. I see what you mean.

CAPTAIN. Yeah?—Well, she *had* 'em! Comparable—to Phoebe's.

PHOEBE. Don't let 'im go on with it, it's just—revoltin'.

CAPTAIN. I says to myself—practicality beginning to win over high idealism—Cornelius Rockley—this porpoise would probably not be a normal boy's first choice—at Frisco Billie's—or even at Alice's place in Santo Domingos—but here, however—

PHOEBE. 'Orrible!

CAPTAIN. Affectations of delicacy! [*One beat—low music begins.*] Swish—swash—swish! Loopin' the loop 'round the raft she goes! All at once—*sssttt!* Very well, Madam! —I reaches out an' I—

PHOEBE. I won't listen to any more— [*Hands to ears.*] -

[CAPTAIN *picks up scratcher from table and starts for her.* PHOEBE *screams. Starts to run out.* HADRIAN *grabs her.*

CAPTAIN *roars—then quiet—puts her back in chair Left.*
HADRIAN *takes scratcher; puts it on table; crosses to door.*
CAPTAIN *sits Right of table.*]

[*Music swells—song ends.*]

REVEREND. Our voices blended very well together.

EMMIE. Didn't they?

MATILDA. It was lovely.

EMMIE. [*Gets chasuble and stole from Left end of desk.*]
Matilda, you play now. I—I have a surprise for Mr. Melton.

REVEREND. [*Crosses down Right of sofa and to between
coffee table and sofa.*] Why, good Heavens! It's a—

EMMIE. Chasuble! Purple for Palm Sunday! And a stole!

REVEREND. [*Genuinely moved.*] Miss Emmie— No!—
You shouldn't!

EMMIE. It's nearly finished. [*She sits down on the sofa
moving decorously aside to give him space beside her.*]

REVEREND. [*Sitting.*] Tell me now— Is Emmie short for
Emmaline—or Emily—or Emma?

EMMIE. [*Looking shyly down.*] Oh, it's—just Emmie.

[MATILDA *plays spinet softly under. Having got the* CAP-
TAIN *relatively settled down in the cabin,* HADRIAN *steals
unobtrusively out with his penny flute. The light has now
grown very dim, there is still a golden afterglow from the
garden against which the figures in the living room are
silhouetted almost like cameos.* HADRIAN *remains in the
archway between the living room and hall, unnoticed by
those in the room and looking on with an air of Pan-like*

secrecy. The CAPTAIN *broods over a problem at the chess-board.*]

REVEREND. My mother's name was Allegra, although she had a very grave disposition.

EMMIE. How long is it since she passed over?

REVEREND. A shorter time than it seems. A year and—let me see—three months. She was born on All Souls Day—she passed away on Epiphany.

EMMIE. You must be—lonely at times.

REVEREND. More than you could understand, Miss Emmie.

EMMIE. Oh, no, I do understand.

REVEREND. We had such a deep spiritual companionship.

EMMIE. Let us hope that—in the course of time—you will find another to almost take her place.

REVEREND. There are so few who are capable of that type of companionship.

EMMIE. Very few, that's true. But there are some.

REVEREND. Our bodies are an obstruction.

EMMIE. I've also had that feeling.

REVEREND. Have you?—Well—how strange! [*Slight pause.*] The rectory as you know is a very large building. And your dealings with that obstreperous gardener of yours are little or nothing to the nerve-wracking difficulties that I have had with servants.

EMMIE. I've said to myself so often, "Mr. Melton is undertaking too much with his—delicate physique!"

REVEREND. No, I haven't been well. I have a little cardiac condition.

EMMIE. Organic?

REVEREND. Just functional, I believe. They call it neuro-circulatory—asthenia.

EMMIE. You won't take care of yourself. You need some-body to shoulder responsibilities for you.

REVEREND. Yes, but I have so little hope of finding another person—a woman—who shares my distaste for the carnal —physical—bodily side of—

EMMIE. I know what you mean.

REVEREND. To be capable of a companionship of spirit.

EMMIE. Oh, but there are such women.

REVEREND. Where?

EMMIE. I can only judge by the fact that what you desire is what I desire, Mr. Melton.

REVEREND. A purely—?

EMMIE. Spiritual companionship! [*They glance at each other with shy hope.*]

REVEREND. What I look for in—home life—is not excite-ment but a—

EMMIE. Sustaining tranquility?

REVEREND. Yes!!—On sunny mornings—a little work in the garden. Afterwards—teas—social calls—

EMMIE. Meetings! And after dinner?

REVEREND. A quiet hour of music. Then he to his study for contemplation—

EMMIE. And—she?

REVEREND. To her books, her sewing.

EMMIE. To meet refreshed at—?

REVEREND. At *breakfast!* [*Their eyes meet in breathless understanding.*] Now you tell me what you look for.

EMMIE. The same!

[*In the cabin* PHOEBE *has nodded at the table—her head is down on her arms. Suddnly the* CAPTAIN *prods her with the back-scratcher. She springs up shrieking. He prods her again and she plunges wildly out of the cabin door—the* CAPTAIN *after her.*]

PHOEBE. [*Dashing across the hall.*] Stop it! Stop it! Mr. Rockley! You know I can't stand it! [*Appeals to* HA-DRIAN.] Mr. 'Adrian, make him stop it!

EMMIE. [*Hurrying to the hall.*] Phoebe!

PHOEBE. He's ticklin' me again, Ma'am, and I won't stand it any longer. [*She dashes into the kitchen.*]

CAPTAIN. Come back here! Come back here y' imp of Satan. Y'r bustin' up the tea-party, youh silly bitch!

EMMIE. *Cornelius!* [EMMIE *breaks down and hurries up-stairs, sobbing.*]—Cornelius! How could you?

[MR. MELTON *rises, aghast. The* CAPTAIN *goes slowly back into the cabin.*]

REVEREND. [*To* MATILDA.] Mr. Rockley?

MATILDA. Yes.

REVEREND. I can assure you the situation is quietly and sympathetically understood in the parish.

MATILDA. [*Looking up without hope.*] Is it? I was afraid it must be.

REVEREND. I—I—I—just remembered—I have a sick call to make. Dear me! Nearly six! You will give my apologies and my thanks for a lovely tea to your dear aunt. I'll expect you both at choir practice tomorrow.

MATILDA. Yes. Thank you. Goodbye. You can go out this way.

[*She indicates the garden exit, as the* REVEREND *pauses timorously.*]

REVEREND Ah—yes— Thank you. [*He goes very quickly.*]

[MATILDA *covers her face and sits at spinet.* HADRIAN *fills his pipe in apparent calm.* EMMIE *gasps and mustering her courage, comes back into room. With tragic perception she stares at the silent tableau.*]

EMMIE. [*In a queer voice.*] Matilda! Mr. Melton—gone?

MATILDA. [*Hoarsely.*] Yes—gone.

[EMMIE *moves lifelessly toward stairs.*]

HADRIAN. [*With true sympathy, touching her elbow.*] Don't, Aunt Emmie.

EMMIE. [*Wildly, turning upon him.*] Leave me alone, don't speak to me! Everything's been ruined. [*She turns and runs upstairs.*]

HADRIAN. [*To* MATILDA, *who still sits at the spinet, her head on her hands.*] Had she expectations about the preacher?

[MATILDA *does not answer. He extends his hand to touch her shoulder, but she draws back.*]

CAPTAIN. [*Staggers out. He looks contritely up the stairs.* EMMIE *can be heard sobbing above. He shuffles into the living room.*] Matilda, Hadrian. The bird of remorse—has got his beak in my heart.

CURTAIN

ACT TWO

ACT TWO

SCENE I

SCENE : *Late that evening.*
The CAPTAIN *and* HADRIAN *are alone in the house. The*
CAPTAIN, *still dishevelled, has plunged into drunken gloom*
and is marching about the house like a King Lear in dun-
garees, with his bottle and glass.
HADRIAN *stands at the French doors.*

CAPTAIN. Yes, yes, yes! The bitter old bird of remorse has
got his beak in my heart. [*Raises his glass.*] Empty—like
my existence. Watchman! What of the night? [*Hand to
head.*] Oh—

HADRIAN. The moon is scudding in and out of the clouds
like it was chased by something. [*Parts the curtains.*]

CAPTAIN. Ahh!

HADRIAN. Hey—Captain!

CAPTAIN. What?

HADRIAN. They're coming back. It's stopped raining, but
Matilda has got the umbrella up.

CAPTAIN. Now I'll catch it. Hadrian, stand by me. We'll
put up a solid front. [*Contradicting his brave assertion, he
backs out into the hall.*]

HADRIAN. Maybe the moon, or the meeting, has drawn
their acid out and made them forgiving.

45

CAPTAIN. Not Emmie. She'll never forgive me for driving off that little ecclesiastical capon.

[*They go into the cabin.* EMMIE *and* MATILDA *enter by the front door.*]

EMMIE. I didn't have much heart for the Athenaeum. Thank Heavens there were so few there—seventeen!

MATILDA. Eighteen, I think.

EMMIE. Miss Cole doesn't count. Only goes to meetings because her house isn't heated and falls asleep the moment she hits the chair. Right in the middle of reading my paper all I could see or hear was that horrid servant bursting out of the Captain's cabin—shrieking—"Miss Emmie 'e's ticklin' me, m'um!"—and just when Mr. Melton had come to the point of—

MATILDA. Aunt Emmie, did Mr. Melton really propose?

EMMIE. Why do you ask that so doubtfully? Does it seem inconceivable that I could be desirable as a wife?

MATILDA. Oh, no, Aunt Emmie.

EMMIE. He visualized the very beautiful and unusual sort of life we were going to have together.

MATILDA. Well, you'll still have it together.

EMMIE. No. Not after what happened here this afternoon.

MATILDA. Poor father was not himself, you realize that.

EMMIE. I realize he was goaded by that—

MATILDA. Aunt Emmie, please try to get it off your mind so you can sleep— I'm going upstairs.

EMMIE. Yes, go on up, Matilda.

MATILDA. Aren't you coming up?

EMMIE. Not immediately. [HADRIAN *opens the cabin door a crack.*] It doesn't take a detective to guess that someone's been sprawling on this sofa. [*Plumps cushion and crosses to Right end of the desk. Sees broken pieces of statue on floor Right of desk.*] My Winged Victory! [HADRIAN *closes door.*] Look where it was. My Winged Victory! [*Up to steps.*] It's no use trying to keep nice things in a house with people who don't respect nice things, and people who don't respect nice things in a house have no respect for anything, mortal or divine. No! They are all for change in the world. And what change?—Blowing up! Smashing! Devastation!

CAPTAIN. Who is she talking to?

HADRIAN. Herself.

CAPTAIN. I doubt it.

[HADRIAN *indicates* CAPTAIN *should snore.*]

EMMIE. Hmph! Hadrian, I can smell your pipe through the door and as for that snoring of the Captain's—nothing could be less convincing.

CAPTAIN. Emmie—

EMMIE. [*Reverting to martyrdom.*] I'm much too deeply, deeply hurt to scold you, Cornelius. Your own conscience is what you will have to answer to tonight. [*She starts for the stairs.*]

CAPTAIN. Emmie—

EMMIE. Yes?

CAPTAIN. [*Coming to cabin door and drawing it open.*] The bird of remorse—has really got his beak in my heart!

EMMIE. Has he, indeed! He must have a very dull beak. Hadrian, I'm sure the Captain needs rest after his strenuous efforts this afternoon. You had better go upstairs and leave him to sleep.

HADRIAN. Yes, Emmie.

EMMIE. Don't just say, "yes, Emmie," and keep him up for the rest of the night with your—your—your eloquent talk about the future.

HADRIAN. [*Coming to the door.*] I'm sorry I talked too much.

EMMIE. Well—it won't hurt you to talk a little bit more. Come into the living room, Hadrian. Cornelius, go right to bed and rest your legs. [*She closes the cabin door.*]

[HADRIAN *follows her into the living room.*]

CAPTAIN. Don't scold Hadrian, Emmie. He can't help I'm a rascal.

EMMIE. Huh! [*She turns on a lamp in the living room and draws the drapes to the hall.*]

HADRIAN. [*Settling himself carelessly on sofa.*] How was the meeting?

EMMIE. That's not what I want to talk about. I have a few things to say to you. You've changed a great deal. It's gratifying to see how much you've come out—the commission—the decoration—we're all very happy for you. [*Sits in chair Left of sofa.*]

HADRIAN. Thank you, Emmie.

EMMIE. However, you still have that grin.

HADRIAN. A charity boy's defense, I guess.

EMMIE. When you were here before you held your tongue. But this afternoon! Heavens! What talk! You grin like a schoolboy and tell how the world should be run.

HADRIAN. Out with it, Aunt Emmie. You want me to leave.

EMMIE. My brother's health can't stand these dissipations for even a short time. Every little excitement makes him drink. He took to drinking the minute he learned you were coming. Also Matilda—she finds your presence disturbing. I am rather worried about her vagueness.

HADRIAN. So am I.

EMMIE. It's no concern of yours.

HADRIAN. It is.

EMMIE. Why?

HADRIAN. I'm very fond of her.

EMMIE. Nonsense! Stop pretending!

HADRIAN. Father drinks more than ever and Matilda has taken to dreams. It must be because they're neither well satisfied with the life in this place.

EMMIE. You sound as if you were blaming me. Even you must know what I am—a living sacrifice here. How long did you plan to stay here?

HADRIAN. Oh, just—long enough—

EMMIE. For what? What are you up to?

HADRIAN. [*Nods sympathetically.*] Up to?

EMMIE. I know you're up to something. Oh, don't pretend it's affection. You never had any.

HADRIAN. How do you know that?

EMMIE. You were here five years, a silent, grinning boy—sly, like a fox—who suddenly sneaked off without a word. Now you come back—a jack-in-the-box, when we thought you'd gone for good. What is it you want? Money? You're not even legally adopted. However, I happen to know that my brother intends you to have a hundred pounds or so. I think it could be arranged to give it to you now. That is, when you leave. Dame Willoughby has offered to drive you back to London with her day after tomorrow.

HADRIAN. That's sooner than I planned to go.

EMMIE. You have no reason to stay on here at all. You don't fit in. You have the usual class resentment of persons in your situation.

HADRIAN. What *is* my situation, Aunt Emmie?

EMMIE. You have no background but what we tried to give you the five years you spent here.   -

HADRIAN. There you're mistaken. It's true my origin's not a very clear one. I was left on the front steps of a foundling home—that's true. [*He grins.*] I was presented to the world, you might say! And so the world is my background.

EMMIE. A very cosmopolitan one, to be sure.

HADRIAN. That's right. I grew up reaching for something that wasn't there any more—maybe the breast of my mother!

EMMIE. [*Disgustedly.*] Uhhhhhh!

HADRIAN. Something warm and able to give me comfort— .
I guess that's what I'm still reaching for. To be warmed—touched—loved! Five years I tried for that here. I got no more than those clay pots in the sheds. After I left here I learned the ways that you get along in the world—working

hard and facing things straight—but still I had that long-ing, not satisfied yet. To be touched. Now I feel that need more than ever. *That's* why I came back here for a second try.

EMMIE. A play for sympathy.

HADRIAN. No.

EMMIE. Even if you mean that—surely you're able to see there's no one here but the sick old man in the study who cares any more for you than—any clay pot in the shed as you aptly put it. *That* you can take my word for.

HADRIAN. No, I can't and I won't take your word for it. I'm very happy and grateful that Father cares for me—but that's not all the pottery house has to offer.

EMMIE. An honest confession! You *have* come back for money.

HADRIAN. I want no money.

EMMIE. You *are* up to something. Yes! You're plotting.

HADRIAN. Right!

EMMIE. What is it?

HADRIAN. [*Grinning.*] Wait and see.

EMMIE. [*Rising.*] Ah, that grin, that detestable grin! Only a person as basely born as you are could have so little pride as to want to stay on in a place he knows he's not wanted. Uhh! I'll tell you good night. [*She starts for the stairs.*]

CAPTAIN. [*Bursts out of the cabin and faces her in the hall with a drunken glare.*] I'm smothered. [*Sudden roar.*]

EMMIE. Cornelius!

CAPTAIN. Tear down the walls.

EMMIE. Hush! You'll be heard in the rectory.

CAPTAIN. Tear down the walls, I'm suffocating in here. Hadrian!

HADRIAN. Yes, Father?

CAPTAIN. You're strong, you can do it—*do it.* I'm choking on old dry dust that fills a place when it's shut.

EMMIE. Unless you are still, I shall call and get the male nurse. To bring the strait-jacket. [CAPTAIN *covers his face.*] We *shall* have some peace around here! [*She goes on up the stairs and out of sight.*]

CAPTAIN. [*Mockingly.*] We *shall* have some peace around here. [*He strikes his thighs with his fists.*] My fathers were navigators. Men who sailed many seas! [*Crying out.*] Here's where they end— [*Sobbing.*] The whole wild raging crew end here in this old shut-down pottery house. Here's where their blood stops, boy. Here's where it stops. In two locked, stagnant pools—my sister Emmie and my daughter Matilda! And in *me*—this drunken old—mongrel! This howler, this monster! This frightener-of-ministers-away! Here—stops—all!! You see? Once I wanted life badly. Me—a navigator also. I was the Captain of the Polar Star. What a proud vessel! She only regretted the sky was not also an ocean that she could sail in, too. Yeah, she would have liked to sail through the constellations, she wouldn't have stopped till the edge of the universe. But I—I traded her in for a barrel of rum, took on at the Port of Jamaica. [*He bursts into bitter laughter.*] Piled her up—lost my papers—Uhhh—I need a drink. [*He staggers into the cabin followed by* HADRIAN.] Here's my Polar Star in a pottery house! [*Turns the wheel.*] You take the dog-watch, boy, I'll mind the wheel. I wasn't always a soft old man like this. I once—you know what I did? I took up an axe and went in the pottery sheds and smashed up all the pots.

HADRIAN. Yes?

CAPTAIN. A useless sort of resistance. You see, there was so much more and more and more of lifeless clay on the place than there was rage in a former sailor. The very next morning the broken pots were replaced by nice little new ones. The vast accumulation went on and on without any more interruptions. You see, the place now, locked up—shut down—lifeless. Windows covered with vines. Doors barred. A privet hedge. A double row of petunias— A great big mirror for us to look at ourselves in. How could anything living get through such obstructions? Impossible!

HADRIAN. [*Gently, touching his shoulder.*] It's time for bed.

CAPTAIN. Eh?

HADRIAN. Bed. I sleep upstairs?

CAPTAIN. Oh, no, you don't. I sleep top-side tonight. You sleep down here in the cabin of the Polar Star.

HADRIAN. But this is your bunk, Captain.

CAPTAIN. Tonight it's yours. Why, if I let you sleep up there on the weather-deck my virtuous sister would murder you in your bed.

HADRIAN. You think you can make the stairs?

CAPTAIN. [*Comes out of cabin.*] I'd climb the mizzen-mast if I'd a mind to. [*He climbs stairs painfully.*] Home is the sailor, home from the sea—and the hunter, home from the hill! [*He climbs out of sight.*]

[HADRIAN *looks after him from the hall. He shakes his head, turns out the hall light and goes into the cabin. He opens the drapes to let the moonlight in and lies down on the bed. After a moment a disturbance is heard outside. The fox is making another foray on the hen yard.* FLORA *barks in her basket. The chickens set up a wild clamor. Dogs on neighboring farms add distant alarms.* EMMIE *suddenly rounds the turn of the stairs in extreme agitation. She wears a black robe and her hair is in curlers.* MATILDA *opens her door on the landing.*]

MATILDA. The fox?

EMMIE. *Yes!* [*She darts down the stairs to kitchen hall and grabs up the shotgun.*]

MATILDA. Aunt Emmie, be careful!

EMMIE. This is one invasion that I can stop. [*She rushes out the French doors without even turning on a light. The clamor continues a few moments. Two shots ring out.*]

[MATILDA *gasps and descends the stairs in her night dress. She looks Ophelia-like and lovely in the dim light.* HADRIAN *on the other side of the partition rises from bed and crosses silently to the door, which he leaves closed. He stands listening.*]

EMMIE. [*After a second, comes back in as furiously as she left.*] Well, at least I've scared him away.

MATILDA. Oh, you *missed* him!

EMMIE. [*Replacing gun in kitchen hall.*] Yes. It's useless—Close the door and get on back to bed. [*She starts upstairs grimly.*]

MATILDA. [*Looking at the cabin door.*] You've probably waked up Father.

[EMMIE *mounts out of sight.* MATILDA *hears a light sound from the cabin where she presumes her father is sleeping as usual.*]

MATILDA. Father? [HADRIAN *smiles and retreats noiselessly to bed.* MATILDA *pushes open the door gently and slips in.*] Father? Did it wake you? [HADRIAN *does not answer and she advances to the side of the bed. She extends her hand and touches his forehead.*] Your forehead is hot. Have you fever?

HADRIAN. [*Stirring.*] No, Matilda.

MATILDA. [*Starts, profoundly shocked.*] Hadrian? You here? I—thought you were—*Father!*

[HADRIAN *laughs uncomfortably. Both of them feel an unreasonable embarrassment over the simple mistake.* MATILDA *gasps and runs quickly out of the cabin, slamming the door. On the other side of the partition, she leans weakly against the newel post of the stairs. The windows give moonlight on her. She seems to be faint with shock. She raises the hand with which she has touched the youth's forehead. She looks down at it and rubs it with a pained expression as if the hand has touched something that scorched it.* HADRIAN, *in the cabin, sits up in the bunk. He turns on the lamp and then gently—gently—he touches with his fingers his forehead where* MATILDA *placed her inadvertent caress, the first he has felt since the almost-a-dream of his mother.*]

CURTAIN

ACT TWO

Scene II

Scene: *The following morning. The breakfast corner is brilliantly lighted by the morning sun pouring through the leaded glass windows. A pearly glow falls over the table, and the green leaves can be seen quivering outside.*
Phoebe *is setting the table.* Matilda *comes downstairs dressed smartly. She is pale and nervous.*

Matilda. Has everyone eaten?

Phoebe. Miss Emmie's 'ad 'ers, but Mr. 'Adrian says 'e'd wait and 'ave 'is breakfast with *you.*

Matilda. Oh.

Phoebe. Wasn't it too bad about the rooster? Miss Emmie says she mistook him for the fox! What a calamity for the female chickens! [*She giggles spasmodically.*]

Matilda. [*Sharply.*] That's enough, Phoebe.

Phoebe. [*Subsiding quickly.*] Yes'm. I'll call in Mr. 'Adrian for 'is breakfast.

Matilda. *No.*

Phoebe. What, Miss?

Matilda. You'll wait to call him until after I've finished my coffee.

Phoebe You don't *want* to eat with 'im?

MATILDA. I happen to be very nervous this morning and I want to have my coffee by myself.

PHOEBE. But 'e'll be disappointed.

MATILDA. Not seriously. What is he—doing now?

PHOEBE. I seen 'im strolling around by the pottery sheds. Oh, it was *so* embarrassing this morning. I didn't have no idea 'e was sleeping in Mr. Rockley's place in the cabin. *So*—when I popped in with the carrot juice, I screamed out loud. 'E was taking 'is exercises. [*She starts out, giggles.*] 'E's very well *built*, Miss.

MATILDA. *Phoebe!* Please bring me my coffee.

[PHOEBE *goes out to the kitchen to fetch the coffee.* HA-DRIAN *quietly enters from the garden.* MATILDA, *curiously panicky, starts to escape outside through the French doors.*]

HADRIAN. [*Crossing quickly.*] Matilda, don't run away. I've waited half an hour to eat with you.

MATILDA. I'm not having breakfast, only a cup of coffee.

HADRIAN. Have it with me.

MATILDA. I'm due at the church in a minute. I promised Miss Tyler I'd go over the Palm Sunday music with her.

PHOEBE. [*Re-entering.*] Coffee for two?

HADRIAN. Yes, please.

PHOEBE. Very good, sir.

HADRIAN. And some toast—and what kind of jelly have you?

PHOEBE. *Mar*—malade! Perfectly delicious—it's orange.

[*Runs excitedly out.*]

MATILDA. [*Is very uncomfortable alone with* HADRIAN, *and keeps her look out the window.*] It's—it's warm for this time of year. [*She speaks stiffly.*]

HADRIAN. Yes, it is. It's weather to walk about in.   .

MATILDA. You've been out walking?

HADRIAN. Yes. I thought you might want to walk a bit, too!

MATILDA. I'd like to do numbers of things that I don't have time to do. I know our lives seem—empty. But we have—various duties.

HADRIAN. [*Gently.*] Sure. I know you do. [*A pause, in which he stares at her. She fidgets.*] I like that dress.

MATILDA. You *always* refer to my clothes.

HADRIAN. Does that—disturb you?   -

MATILDA. Yes. Yes, frankly, it does. Clothes are merely—clothes.

HADRIAN. I understand the fox came back last night.

MATILDA. He did.

HADRIAN. I heard the shooting. Did she miss him?

MATILDA. Unfortunately, she did. She hit the Stoneyfield rooster, the one that got us a ribbon at the Fair.

HADRIAN. [*With a faint smile.*] Well, at least she succeeded in reducing the net amount of masculinity on the place.

MATILDA. I don't imagine that gave her much satisfaction. [*Calls.*] *Phoebe!*

HADRIAN. [*Grinning.*] No?

MATILDA. She's either too fast, or too slow. How long have we been waiting here for her to bring the coffee?

HADRIAN. Not as long as it seems. It seems much longer because you're so embarrassed.

MATILDA. Yes, I *am* embarrassed, that's quite true. [*Picking up a silver spoon to stare at it.*] How long will you stay in England?

HADRIAN. You mean, how long am I going to embarrass you here?

MATILDA. No. I'm used to feeling embarrassed. It doesn't matter. But you—wouldn't you find more pleasure some place else? Pleasures must be important when you're a soldier.

HADRIAN. *This* is pleasure. I'm mean enough to like it, even though it makes you concentrate on a silver teaspoon.

MATILDA. [*Setting the teaspoon down and looking out the window.*] What do you plan to do now the war is over?

HADRIAN. I'll go back to the light and power plant in Montreal.

MATILDA. You seem to belong very much in the new world now. *You* believe in the *future.*

HADRIAN. Yes. Don't you?

MATILDA. Everything that changes scares me a little. Those new frontiers you spoke of—the ones that the brain will extend to enlarge our freedom. Isn't that what you said?

HADRIAN. Yes.

MATILDA. Doesn't that work need your immediate attention?

HADRIAN. [*Quietly.*] The future is not conceited. The future knows the good things in the past. Just as well as it knows the deceit and confusion. It doesn't want to leave everything behind. And so it pauses to look the old things over and pick out one or two—or even three,—that it wants to take along with it. Such things as music—poetry—and gentleness,—Matilda!

MATILDA. What good would such things be in the power plant?

HADRIAN. I think you don't understand what a power plant is. It isn't a hard young man without any feelings.

MATILDA. No?

HADRIAN. It's not an upstart charity boy with nothing but an insolent grin and a pack of ruthless muscles.

MATILDA. No? I supposed that it was.

HADRIAN. What a mistake you made! The future is only fierce for a little while so that after that time it can afford to be gentle. Much more gentle than the wrong, deceitful past of the world could be—could afford to be. Oh, Matilda, Matilda! There's struggle ahead. Let's not sit it out in shut-down pottery houses. If we do, we'll lose—and in the end it won't be possible for even the most determined sitters-out to keep the gentleness in them. They'll lose all they want—to the ones that resist our progress.

MATILDA. You have a way of talking with lots of feeling about such indefinite things that one doesn't get your meaning. I have to go. [*Starts.*]

HADRIAN. Not yet! Matilda, don't run away yet. [*He catches her hand as she starts to leave.*]

MATILDA. I'm going to be late.

HADRIAN. Please stay.

[*Smiles at her winningly. She reluctantly returns.* PHOEBE *enters with the coffee.*]

MATILDA. [*Nervously.*] Why did you wait so long to bring the coffee?

PHOEBE. [*Smiling at* HADRIAN.] I didn't want to interrupt the talk. [*Puts coffee on table.*]

MATILDA. You're always concerned about the wrong things, Phoebe. [*There is the sound of organ music from the church next door.*] I'm already late. Miss Tyler is running over the music now.

[PHOEBE *goes into kitchen.*]

HADRIAN. You're a funny girl.

MATILDA. [*Sits at table. Pouring the coffee.*] What's funny about me?

HADRIAN. [*Sits at table.*] The way you—defeat yourself.

MATILDA. That strikes me as being—a curious remark. What do you mean by it?

HADRIAN. You tell me that I stare at you. I pay you clumsy compliments all the time. It makes you uncomfortable. Well, I can't seem to help it. It's only an awkward mixed-up way of telling you something else.

MATILDA. [*Handing him cup.*] Your coffee.

HADRIAN. Yes, yes, thank you. You see, you're amazingly—gentle.

MATILDA. What?

HADRIAN. Gentle. Delicate.

MATILDA. Oh.

HADRIAN. Why nothing in the world is as gentle as you are. You're as delicately put together as—one of those misty little white cottony things that float around in the sunlight, scarcely seeable, they are so fine and soft. Touch them? You wouldn't dare. It's almost too much to look at them. When I escaped from the prison camp, I had to stick a knife in a guard. As he went down, I saw he was only a kid and just as—gentle—as you are. The life in him yielded as softly as tissue paper. I knew very well that gentle things, such as that boy and you, are made to be gently treated. Barely touched, hardly breathed upon. Look! [*She looks at his outstretched hand.*] Do these impress you as being dangerous fingers? Do they look to be fierce and cruel? [MATILDA *looks away.*] They're not. They wouldn't dare touch you without your permission. And if they did, having secured your permission, they'd do it so lightly, with such respect that they'd draw back the moment they moved forward. They'd be more frightened than you are of using too much pressure—of bruising—or leaving the tiniest scar. I'm a gentle person.

MATILDA. I don't know what you are saying all this for—

HADRIAN. Not—yet? Well,—if you would like me to—

MATILDA. Whatever you do—what you like—is not my concern. We live very quietly here—which is the way we want to. I—I don't know how to cope with new situations.

EMMIE. [*Enters downstairs.*] Matilda, why aren't you with Miss Tyler?

MATILDA. I was delayed. I'm going directly.

EMMIE. [*Calls.*] Phoebe!

PHOEBE. [*Off kitchen.*] Yes, mum! I'm coming.

EMMIE. Has your father had his breakfast?

MATILDA. Not yet, but I think he's stirring.

PHOEBE. [*Entering with tray.*] Yes, Mum?

EMMIE. [*Indicating tray.*] Take this—and put Mr. Rockley's breakfast in his study, immediately.

PHOEBE. Yes, mum. [*Goes Left.*]

EMMIE. [*Calling in cabin.*] Captain!—Cap-tain!

CAPTAIN. [*From upstairs.*] Yes, Emmie?

EMMIE. Phoebe can't wait any longer to serve your breakfast. You'll have to take it now or do without it.—Matilda, you'll be late. Your mother always took complete responsibility for the Palm Sunday music. You must hurry.

HADRIAN. Good morning, Aunt Emmie.

EMMIE. You're not through yet? I'll have my coffee later.

HADRIAN. [*Rising.*] Oh, I'm quite through.

CAPTAIN. [*On landing above.*] Good morning, everybody!

HADRIAN. Captain!

MATILDA. Good morning, Father!

CAPTAIN. Give me a smile, sister Emmie, and tell me how can I atone for my follies.

EMMIE. Adjust your braces.

CAPTAIN. Oh, sorry.—What was all the commotion I heard during the night?

HADRIAN. The fox made a raid on the chicken house.

CAPTAIN. Successful?

HADRIAN. Very. He made off with one and Emmie shot the rooster.

[CAPTAIN *laughs.*]

EMMIE. Are you feeling in such high spirits this morning?

[PHOEBE *exits with tray to cabin.*]

CAPTAIN. Ah, yes, I forgot—the bird of remorse, sister Emmie. Morning, Phoebe!

PHOEBE. Morning, sir.

CAPTAIN. Come along into the cabin, son, while I have my coffee. We've had good shooting here lately. One Stoney-field rooster, a prize one—and one little ecclesiastical capon. [*Entering cabin, calling in to* MATILDA.] Hey, Matilda, you didn't come to tuck me in last night. [*Sits Right of table.*]

MATILDA. I came, Father, but you had moved upstairs without telling me.

CAPTAIN. So you tucked in Hadrian, huh?

HADRIAN. [*Turns and grins at* MATILDA.] Yes—that's what she did. [*Goes into cabin leaving the door open.*]

[MATILDA *flushes.* EMMIE *gives her a sharp look.*]

CAPTAIN. [*Roars with laughter.*] Tucked in the charity boy!

EMMIE. He's started drinking already.

MATILDA. Yes. Oh, Emmie, it's unbearable.

CAPTAIN. [*Shouting from the cabin.*] Come on in here, Matilda, and set down with us.

MATILDA. Can't do it—I'm late for Miss Tyler.

[*She goes to the front door, suddenly remembers something and slams the door shut from inside. She starts for the living room.* HADRIAN'S *voice stops her—she is out of sight, the door of the cabin is just at that angle of openness that conceals her.*]

HADRIAN. [*Sitting Left of the table.*] Hasn't our Matilda any beaux, Father?

CAPTAIN. Nary a one!

HADRIAN. Has she decided to be an old maid?

[MATILDA *clasps her hand to her mouth.*]

CAPTAIN. Probably has. She follows her aunt's example in everything else. [*Sips his coffee.*]

[EMMIE *snorts indignantly and advances a few steps to hear better the conversation. A dual scene is played, the* CAPTAIN *and* HADRIAN *talking in the cabin, unconscious of the partly open door,* EMMIE *and* MATILDA *overhearing in anger and dismay on the other.*]

HADRIAN. I think that Emmie was meant to be an old maid. But Matilda isn't.

CAPTAIN. No?

HADRIAN. She has more tenderness in her.

CAPTAIN. You think so?

HADRIAN. Yes.—She is so full of tenderness that if you touched her she would probably faint. Some women are like that. All of this unspent tenderness grows and grows until it gets to be something enormous. Then finally there is so much of it, it explodes inside them—and they go to pieces.

[MATILDA *utters a stifled cry.* EMMIE *gasps and clutches* MATILDA'S *arm. They stare into each other's faces in rage and horror.*]

CAPTAIN. [*Indulging smile at the earnest young man.*] I'm sorry that you foresee such a bleak fate for Matilda.

HADRIAN. Oh, I don't think that is going to happen to her. I think it can be prevented.

CAPTAIN. Good. You seem to have learned a great deal about women.

HADRIAN. Nope. I know very little. I've had no love affairs, Captain.

CAPTAIN. Hmmm????

HADRIAN. No.—I'm glad now that I haven't,—that all of that feeling inside me hasn't been touched—it makes a finer thing to give to a woman.

EMMIE. [*In a furious whisper.*] Listen! The peacock! The puffed up little—

CAPTAIN. Then you must choose a woman.

HADRIAN. I have chosen one.

CAPTAIN. Already? [HADRIAN *nods.*] When?

HADRIAN. Last night.

[EMMIE *has turned away from* MATILDA. *Now she slowly faces her and the horrified, prolonged stare is resumed.*]

CAPTAIN. [*Slowly setting down the coffee cup.*] *Last night?*

HADRIAN. Yes.

CAPTAIN. I didn't know that you left the house last night.

HADRIAN. I didn't leave the house—it happened here.

CAPTAIN. Here? In the pottery house? [HADRIAN *nods.*] *What* happened? Go on! Go on! What are you talking about?

HADRIAN. I found her here.

EMMIE. Merciful Heavens!

HADRIAN. Last night.

MATILDA. Aunt Emmie!

HADRIAN. In the pottery house.

[PHOEBE *enters and goes into the cabin with the* CAPTAIN'S *breakfast.*]

CAPTAIN. [*Grinning up at* PHOEBE.] Don't tell me you've set your cap at Phoebe.

[PHOEBE *hurries out to the kitchen.*]

HADRIAN. No, not Phoebe.

CAPTAIN. Who, then?

HADRIAN. *Matilda!*

[*At the mention of her name,* MATILDA *gasps as if struck.*]

CAPTAIN. [*Suddenly grave.*] What? Your sister?

HADRIAN. She isn't my sister. We're not blood relations.

CAPTAIN. That I know—but—when did this enter your mind?

HADRIAN. I just told you. Last night.

CAPTAIN. What in God's name put it into your head?

HADRIAN. I told you that, too. Matilda came in here.

[CAPTAIN *suddenly chuckles.*]

MATILDA. [*Has turned about in panic. She starts for the cabin door.* EMMIE *clutches her shoulders. They cling together in the hallway.*] Aunt Emmie, Aunt Emmie!

EMMIE. Keep hold of yourself. Just wait! [*She marches to the cabin door and stands poised for the attack.*]

CAPTAIN. She came in here?

HADRIAN. Yes. I'd just put out the light. She entered the room and she came over to the bed and she touched me.

EMMIE. [*With a loud and furious outcry she sweeps the door open and plunges into the cabin.*] A lie! An outrageous lie! [MATILDA *throws up her arms in a shuddering motion. She stifles a cry and shrinks back against the dark corner of the hall.*] Cornelius, are you utterly insane? How can you let him speak such a loathsome lie?

HADRIAN. [*Rising politely.*] Won't you sit down, Emmie.

EMMIE. [*Turning upon him.*] You!

CAPTAIN. Don't interrupt, Emmie—you're intruding.

EMMIE. Intruding? *I'm* not the intruder.

CAPTAIN. Yes, you are. You're butting in. Go on, Hadrian, what were you going to say?

HADRIAN. I've just about said what I was going to say. I would like to—marry—our—Matilda.

EMMIE. [*Faces the* CAPTAIN.] Now you see what comes of taking in strangers. When this unmentionable thing was a child of ten you thrust him on us and we endured him five years. That was enough—enough! This is a little too much.

CAPTAIN. [*Furiously.*] Emmie, your mouth is spitting toads. Shut up!

EMMIE. His mouth is spitting toads! Didn't you hear what he said of our Matilda? He said she came to his room!

HADRIAN. She came by accident, mistake. She didn't know her father had gone upstairs. But still—she touched me.

EMMIE. If *I* had touched you, I would cut off my hand.

HADRIAN. You are not Matilda.

EMMIE. She would have cut it off, too, before she ever would have let it touch you on purpose.

HADRIAN. That I don't know. I think it remains to be seen.

[MATILDA *weakly shuts the front door and leans exhausted against it with a hand pressed to her throat.*]

EMMIE. [*Bursts into mocking laughter.*] You think we're two silly spinsters so starved for attention that even an illegitimate upstart—like you can turn our heads in order to get what he is after.

CAPTAIN. [*Catching at her wrist.*] Hadrian is my son.

EMMIE. Matilda is your daughter. Are you—mad?

CAPTAIN. I warn you—watch your tongue.

EMMIE. It wasn't enough you destroyed my life with your drunkenness, drove Mr. Melton out of the house yesterday afternoon just as he was about to ask me to—

CAPTAIN. To what? What would that be? Two zeroes make a zero. What would you and the Reverend Mr. Melton produce?

EMMIE. *Oh—you—disgusting—!*

CAPTAIN. A man wants his blood to go on, not be dried up in a stagnant little pool of—holy water.

EMMIE. Uhhh! I see now. You did it on purpose. [*Turning on* HADRIAN.] You, too! You conspired together. You wrecked my life and now you want to wreck Matilda's.

CAPTAIN. No! Hadrian has proposed a plan to save her.

EMMIE. A plan? Oh, yes, a plan! I knew you were up to something, I told you I did, last night. However, I did give you credit for having more common charity-boy sense about you than daring to dream you could get what you're after through using our Matilda.

HADRIAN. What do you think I'm after?

EMMIE. I think you are after—money! The news of the Captain's ill health brought you back like a vulture.

CAPTAIN. Be still, you!

EMMIE. Oh, yes, that was it. But what a fool you are! Our Matilda wouldn't—wouldn't have you if you were the last man alive.

CAPTAIN. Emmie—she will have him.

EMMIE. You poor deluded old man, hoaxed by this trickster. Do you think—our Matilda's a piece of wood to be passed around as you please?

HADRIAN. Look! Our Matilda won't have me, unless she *wants* me.

EMMIE. *Wants* you? Huh!

HADRIAN. Why shouldn't she want me? I'm lonely and looking about for love—and so is she.

EMMIE. [*Quietly to the* CAPTAIN.] Tell him to get out of my house.

CAPTAIN. It isn't your house, it's mine. I want him to stay.

EMMIE. He has no right to anything that's here.

CAPTAIN. [*Meaningly.*] That can be corrected.

EMMIE. What do you mean?

CAPTAIN. I am not without blame as you are—but I plan to rectify my wrongdoings.

EMMIE. Everyone knows that you're a drunken, irresponsible old man who has made a living sacrifice of his family.

CAPTAIN. Either she will have him, or neither of you will get one cent of mine when I'm gone. I will have it fixed in my will that everything goes to Hadrian unless Matilda marries him while I'm living. And you'll get nothing—not even the pots in the shed. Maybe now you'll stop your efforts to keep life out of the place. I'll see my lawyer. See my lawyer.

[EMMIE *rushes hysterically out, turns around like a headless chicken—snatches up her coat from rack.*]

MATILDA. What are you going to do?

EMMIE. [*Running toward front door.*] I'm going to see Mr. Melton! Stay here! Be calm! [*Exits in panicky rush.*]

[MATILDA *crosses to the sofa.*]

HADRIAN. [*Peeks out of cabin door.*] Matilda overheard—

CAPTAIN. How does she take it?

HADRIAN. I think she's a little surprised.

CAPTAIN. [*Peeks out, too.*] Sometimes you have to lead a horse to water, and stick its head in the trough and then hold it under until it's willing to drink.

[*He stalks into the living room and stops short, seeing*

MATILDA. *She catches her breath and sobs.* CAPTAIN *grunts and goes upstairs.*]

HADRIAN. [*Steps through the cabin door—moves over toward her.*] Matilda, what are you crying about? [MATILDA *shakes her head.*] Shall I tell you? You're crying for things you've locked yourself away from. You're in danger, Matilda.

MATILDA. [*Weakly.*] Yes, it seems that I am, when even my own father turns against me.

HADRIAN. He is for you, Matilda. And so am I.

MATILDA. I am not a stick of wood—

HADRIAN. No, but you're nearly that lifeless.

MATILDA. Not to be passed around like a stick of wood!

HADRIAN. What you're doing now is worse than that.

MATILDA. Don't come near me.

HADRIAN. *I'm* not the danger.

MATILDA. You *are*. I've always been afraid of you.

HADRIAN. I know that.

MATILDA. When you were a boy you never opened your mouth for more than a word. Your silence was frightening to me. When you sat and stared at me across the table, I dropped my knife and fork and left the table. When I had to pass you on the stairs—I was afraid that you would reach out and stop me—bar the way—so that I couldn't go up or down. I didn't know why. I thought I was being silly. For five years you watched me—watched me. What were you thinking about? I didn't know.

HADRIAN. I was thinking of you. I did stare at you across the table and I was silent because my throat was so tight that I couldn't speak. And when I passed you upon the stairs—I did want to do what you feared I would do— reach out and bar the way. It was only your frightened look that stopped me. But why were you frightened? There is only one danger for you,—the horrible noiseless danger of locked up places. Now that the shrieking pottery girls have gone and the plant's shut down—you find it restful. You like it better this way. You actually hope that the plant won't be re-opened, and it won't be, Matilda. The stillness, the privet hedge, the double row of petunias, the occasional calls of the little parson, will be all. All the grilles and shutters and curtains at the windows and bolts on the doors upstairs and down—they give you a sense of protection. But the world is only dangerous when it is locked out. [MATILDA *starts to rush upstairs.*] Go! Go back upstairs! You'll stay there for good, a little girl grown old still playing with dolls. [*He catches her fingers and holds her from flight.*] Matilda, there's new powers being set loose in the world. New wonders, new thrills, new excitements! I whisper it to you because it is—still a secret!

MATILDA. You—talk insanely!

HADRIAN. And here's something else I whisper to you, Matilda—last night—you touched me!

MATILDA. I touched you by mistake.

HADRIAN. But just the same, you touched me.

MATILDA. What if I did? I touch a lot of things—keys of the piano, the knobs on doors, handles of tea cups. What's the importance of that?

HADRIAN. [*Taking her arms.*] Those things aren't alive.

I'm alive, Matilda. Can't you feel the life that's in my fingers? I felt the warmth and tenderness in yours—when they touched my forehead last night.

MATILDA. An—accident.

HADRIAN. Whether by accident or on purpose, you won't be able to forget it.

MATILDA. [*Breaking away from him with sudden violence.*] Let go of me—you.—Oh, I heard what was said in the cabin—all of it.

HADRIAN. I'm glad you heard it.

MATILDA. I'd cut my hand off before I would touch you on purpose.

HADRIAN. Poor little Matilda. Using words her Aunt Emmie put in her mouth.

MATILDA. They're my words, too.

HADRIAN. No, they're not. Don't you know what your words are? Your words are—loneliness—tenderness— longing—*love!*

EMMIE. [*Enters through the front door.*] Matilda, go up to your room!

[MATILDA *starts.*]

HADRIAN. Stay here, Matilda!

[*She hesitates.*]

EMMIE. Matilda! Go to your room!

HADRIAN. Don't be ordered, Matilda.

EMMIE. Matilda, I'm warning you. You've had a terrible shock and you don't know what you are doing.

HADRIAN. That's a lie.

EMMIE. Matilda—go upstairs! [MATILDA *turns away and goes.*] A pretty compliment you've paid Matilda. You have a few days leave—so you grab at a woman. Matilda happens to be on hand—it's for her you reach. About as flattering as being whistled at from the entrance to a pub. I'm sure she appreciates it.—What a devil you are.

HADRIAN. It takes a devil to contend with a devil. You and I are crossing swords.

EMMIE. I have the stronger weapon—decency on my side.

HADRIAN. Have you enlisted the little parson then?

EMMIE. Yes, he and others. The town will be up in arms against you. You'll be driven off without a single penny.

HADRIAN. I want no money. What I want is Matilda.

EMMIE. That detestable smirk—that grin, you—

HADRIAN. Charity Boy.—Now I must go in town to get the license. [*He pauses on the threshold of front door.*] —Lilies in the garden! Why, they'll be just the thing for the bride's bouquet!

[PHOEBE *enters from kitchen.*]

EMMIE. They'll decorate the church on Easter Sunday! You —arrogant—little—[*Slams the door on him.*] bastard!

CURTAIN

ACT THREE

.

ACT THREE

SCENE I

SCENE: *Late that night. A single lamp burns in the living room where* EMMIE *is dozing in armchair Right Center with a copy of "The Watch and Ward" on her lap.*
PHOEBE *comes in from the kitchen with a doleful expression and lagging steps. She carries a telegram.*

PHOEBE. Oh, Miss Emmie!

EMMIE. [*Awaking with a start.*] What's the matter with you?—What have you there?

PHOEBE. A wire. For the young Lieutenant.

EMMIE. For Hadrian?

PHOEBE. My young man, 'Arry, got one like this when 'e was on leave from 'is boat. Up 'e 'opped in the middle of the night and back to 'is boat, without even stoppin' to—

EMMIE. Put the wire down.

[PHOEBE *places the wire on the desk and goes back to the kitchen.* EMMIE *picks up the wire and tries to fathom its contents. Turns it over several times, tempted to open it as* MATILDA'S *door opens. She is breathtakingly lovely in a delicate, filmy blue-green dress and a pair of feather slippers. She tiptoes down the steps and into the living room.*]

EMMIE. [*Abruptly, putting the wire aside.*] Matilda! I thought we agreed that you were to stay in your room.

79

MATILDA. Haven't they both gone out?

EMMIE. They've gone to the Carnival, but unless they get too drunk to navigate, they'll return to the house.

MATILDA. Well, I can't stay locked in my room indefinitely.

EMMIE. I've reason to think you won't need to stay there much longer. This wire has just come for the military hero. I think it is likely to mean his early departure.

MATILDA. Hadrian's leaving?

EMMIE. In all probability—the result of prayer! In the meantime, there's no reason for you to trail about downstairs in that preposterous outfit.

MATILDA. [*Almost sharply.*] There is no reason for me to do anything, Aunt Emmie!

EMMIE. I see that you're still unnerved from what you've been through. You're shivering. Put this about you. [*Offers her the shawl.*] You mustn't feel insecure. I am here and you are well protected.

MATILDA. [*Taking the shawl from her and replacing it on the sofa.*] I wonder if protection is what I need. When I was a little girl I used to be afraid so often and I always wanted to step inside that big armoire in my room and close the door on myself—it gave me such a warm, protected feeling. Just now, tonight, I had that impulse again. Only this time I knew it wasn't right. Aunt Em, we can't stay on in this shut-down pottery house the rest of our lives.

EMMIE. [*Carefully—alarmed.*] Whoever said we would? As soon as we're relieved of our present responsibilities, you and I will take a long holiday.

MATILDA. Relieved of—you mean—the Captain?

EMMIE. I didn't intend to tell you this—but in our little talk this afternoon, Mr. Melton mentioned a wonderful institute for the care of alcoholics. Once they're admitted, they're not released until a permanent cure has been effected.

MATILDA. You mean—?

EMMIE. Mr. Melton's reaction to what he saw in this house yesterday afternoon was not disgust, but sympathetic concern. "Oh, my dear Miss Emmie," he said again and again. "You and your delicate niece *immured* with that—monster!"

MATILDA. The Captain? A monster? That's a very nasty thing to say.

EMMIE. What we love is the memory of a better man, Matilda. Until that better man is restored, all we can feel is pain and grief and disgust. A man who would dispose of his daughter like a piece of goods to any drinking companion. And if we don't give in to him, turn over all that would have been ours to *him*. [*She sniffs.*]

MATILDA. That's the way it's going to be fixed in the will?

EMMIE. That's the way it could be fixed in the will.

MATILDA. Aunt Emmie—

EMMIE. Yes?

MATILDA. I can't figure it out. Why does Hadrian want me, if he's mercenary? If he doesn't get me all the property and the money goes to him. If he does all he gets *is* me and nothing else.

EMMIE. Back of everything in his mind is the ugliest of human motives—avarice.

MATILDA. No!

EMMIE. I had a talk with him last night after you'd gone to bed. I told him that all I could offer to buy him off was a few hundred pounds or so. It was not enough.

MATILDA. I don't understand. For what?

EMMIE. For giving up his outrageous intentions!

MATILDA. Toward me?

EMMIE. Toward you, toward your father, toward this unlucky house he came into. Now I've told you the story.

MATILDA. I can't believe you.

EMMIE. Matilda, are you suggesting that I'm a liar?

MATILDA. Aunt Emmie, no, no, but—that's so—shocking.

EMMIE. I wanted to spare you the knowledge, but your gullible attitude *forced* me to have you know it. Now, dear, you must go to bed. Have you taken your sleeping pill yet?

MATILDA. No—

EMMIE. Then, take it!

MATILDA. Everything's—broken to pieces.

EMMIE. No. Security is the important thing. We have that here and you may be sure we'll keep it. [*The* CAPTAIN *and* HADRIAN'S *voices are heard, singing a nautical ballad as they approach the front door.*] Quickly, go up to your room! They're coming!—There's no reason for you to see Hadrian again.—[*Hurrying* MATILDA *upstairs and to her door.*] Hurry!

[*As* MATILDA *closes her door the* CAPTAIN *and* HADRIAN *enter.*]

HADRIAN. Hi! Emmie!

[EMMIE *gives them a long and tigerish look and passes with supreme dignity up the stairs and down the corridor to her room.*]

CAPTAIN. That look, my boy, is known as the bar-keeper's boon. It's done more to boost the business of the gin-mill than any other factor in existence.

HADRIAN. [*As they come down into the room* HADRIAN *sees the wire. Opens it and reads.*] Hello! I'm out! I'm out! I'm out and away!

CAPTAIN. Away?—When?

HADRIAN. Tomorrow. Early in the morning.

CAPTAIN. Not that soon.

HADRIAN. I've got to. Orders.

CAPTAIN. Then it's tonight or never! For you and Matilda.

HADRIAN. [*Picking up the fancy bedroom slipper from under chair Right Center.*] What's this? Emmie's?

CAPTAIN. Emmie? In a thing like that? You're maligning my sister's character. No, no, that's Matilda's. Why—why, this is a sign. Don't you see? The girl's been out of her room.

HADRIAN. She must have.

CAPTAIN. We scared her back in.

HADRIAN. [*Dolefully.*] When a girl's as scared of a man as she is of me—maybe he'd best give up an' leave her.

CAPTAIN. Sit down! [*Beckons him commandingly.* HA-

DRIAN *sits Right Center*.] I'll have to explain my daughter Matilda to you.

HADRIAN. Can you?

CAPTAIN. Matilda is a virgin.

HADRIAN. That I know.

CAPTAIN. My sister Emmie is also a virgin.

HADRIAN. That I suspected.

CAPTAIN. But there is a difference in their cases. Emmie's virginity is congenital.

HADRIAN. Isn't that mostly the case?

CAPTAIN. No, no, no, a total misapprehension. Virginity is mostly the consequence of bad environment an' unfavorable social conditions. But Emmie's is congenital, and so firmly entrenched—that dynamite couldn't remove it.

HADRIAN. So—

CAPTAIN. In Emmie's opinion, any threat to virginity is a threat to existence. Why, to me it's surprising that Emmie Rockley will even put a teaspoon in a cup.

HADRIAN. How about the Parson's?

CAPTAIN. No threat!—not even a teaspoon. But as for Matilda—Matilda's case is acquired.

HADRIAN. I never heard that a girl could acquire virginity.

CAPTAIN. Exposed to a virulent case of it like Emmie's, the healthiest constitution would be infected. However—here is the rainbow.

HADRIAN. Where?

CAPTAIN. Matilda Rockley was conceived of—The Captain! [*He slaps his chest.*]

Thousands of navigators are in her blood.
Her blood is the only remaining ocean for them.
Altogether th' whole crew of 'em is bawlin',
"Forward, Matilda! Forward, girl! Go forward!"

[*Crouches before* HADRIAN.] It's up to you to make her listen to 'em.

HADRIAN. How will I do that?

CAPTAIN. Here's her slipper. Slip it on 'er foot.

HADRIAN. Through that locked door, I suppose?

CAPTAIN. No, no, no, not through the door. You can't talk to a woman through a closed door. With a woman, the talk is the touch.

HADRIAN. Yep, the touch is the talk. But how am I going to get in there?

[FLORA *barks outside.* HADRIAN *rises.*]

CAPTAIN. Confound that caterpillar dog! What has she flushed?

HADRIAN. [*At French doors.*] The little minister. He's coming to see us?

CAPTAIN. Holy Jehosophat! Emmie's preacher back? Don't let 'im in.

HADRIAN. If he rings, Aunt Emmie will come downstairs.

CAPTAIN. [*Groaning.*] Then *open* it, damn it!—I'll settle his hash this time. [*He marches to the hall with his jaw stuck out and his eyes glaring, his shirt tails hanging out. Opens the front door.*]

REVEREND. [*Appears, hastened by* FLORA'S *attack, breathless, in the front door.*] Gracious—that animal!

HADRIAN. It's only the little Pekinese of the girls.

REVEREND. Whatever it is, it invariably attacks me. Woooo! [CAPTAIN *agreeably surprised, picks up the dog and kisses it, then throws it back out.*] I'm glad you haven't retired. I've meant to call on you before and at an earlier hour, but I've been busy, busy, busy. [*He assumes his brisk manner.*]

CAPTAIN. You sound like a bumble bee.

REVEREND. Well, I *have* delivered a sting where one was well deserved.

HADRIAN. Where was that, Rector?

REVEREND. There is, as you may be aware—a carnival show in the village. They have up great banners—"SEE THE MUSCLE DANCERS"—and—"NATURE'S GREATEST MISTAKE —THE MORPHODITE!"—directly across from the church property! *Directly* across from us! But *I* have secured an *injunction!*—Those who believe that a period of unbridled license—vulgarity and— [*The* CAPTAIN *throws back his head in a rude guffaw.* REVEREND *turning stiffly from one to the other.*] Young man, will you excuse us? I have to talk privately with Mr. Rockley.

HADRIAN. Yes, indeed. I'll take a look at the ice box. [*Goes into the kitchen.*]

CAPTAIN. [*Leads* REVEREND *into the cabin.*] Come up in here. These are the Captain's quarters. Sit down.

REVEREND. Thank you. The Captain?

CAPTAIN. [*Shuts the door and draws the portieres. Grandly.*] I—am the *Captain!* Well— [*Indicates Right chair.* REVEREND *sits.*] I think we have a degree of privacy now. Well, sir?

[*He stands back of the pilot's wheel, which he turns about during the scene, glaring over the top of it at the little* REV-EREND *as though he were navigating through dangerous waters. His scowl and the turning wheel have a discomfiting effect on the visitor.*]

REVEREND. Mr. Rockley, a minister has so many functions in the community, not all agreeable ones.

CAPTAIN. What's on your mind, Rector?

REVEREND. Mr. Rockley, your sister, Miss Emmie, has enjoined me to undertake a mission which is one which I would like to avoid—but since it concerns the welfare of one of my flock, I feel it to be my—ministerial duty.

CAPTAIN. Have a little drink, Rector?

REVEREND. No, thank you.

CAPTAIN. Well—come to the point.

REVEREND. That—that *wheel* thing! Is it necessary?

CAPTAIN. It gives me something to *grip.* Proceed!

REVEREND. [*After a dubious pause.*] It seems the young man visiting in your house—

CAPTAIN. My boy, Hadrian?

REVEREND. Yes! I have been told a really preposterous story, Mr. Rockley, one that I only give credence to, because on a former—unfortunate occasion—I saw you in what *might* be termed a somewhat inebriated condition. And because it came from the lips of dear Miss Emmie, a lady for whom I hold—something more than—esteem.

CAPTAIN. Go on!

REVEREND. I have been told that this young person has exerted a rather unscrupulous influence over your judgment —that you have told your sister that Miss Matilda, quite against her will, must either consent to enter into matrimony with this completely unsuitable young man—or else forfeit her share of her natural legacy—in the event of your —passing away.

CAPTAIN. Well, sir, now I'd like to ask *you*—what do you aim to do about it?

REVEREND. I trust we will not be forced to take any action.

CAPTAIN. But if you were forced to take action, what would that action be?

REVEREND. The action?

CAPTAIN. Yep. The action.

REVEREND. If we are compelled to take any let us hope that it will be of a corrective rather than a punitive nature. Miss Emmie assures me that you have a gentler side to your nature, which has been the victim of that side brought out through drink.

CAPTAIN. She does, eh?

REVEREND. We—I may even say society itself—recognizes the need of salvaging those better sides of nature.

CAPTAIN. How you gonna salvage it?

REVEREND. There are certain Christian retreats—where shipwrecked souls can be restored and repaired.

CAPTAIN. Retreats, huh?

REVEREND. Provisions are made for physical as well as spiritual restitution. It is our hope that—unless your present confusion promptly disappears—you can be prevailed upon to enter such a Christian retreat where you can be—properly cared for.

CAPTAIN. Let's get this straight. *Who's* hoping?

REVEREND. [*Benignly.*] All who are concerned for your welfare, Mr. Rockley.

CAPTAIN. You talk as though there might be quite a few.

REVEREND. On a certain Sunday not long past, those at divine worship across the lane were made aware of an un-Sabbatical goings-on in this house. A certain—uh—*singing,* shall we say—more profane than sacred.

CAPTAIN. Well, let me tell you, them infernal hymn squawkers of yours—

REVEREND. Now, now, Mr. Rockley! Let us curb our tongues. This is not your better nature speaking. Your better nature is crying aloud for this treatment. It's in response to these cries that we have decided upon our course of action.

CAPTAIN. You have decided?

REVEREND. Miss Emmie and I have arrived at a mutual conclusion. We have a place in mind.

CAPTAIN. One of them Christian retreats?

REVEREND. I wrote a letter today making tentative arrangements. All will be taken care of—you need have no fear—unless your present confusion and its cause promptly disappear.

CAPTAIN. The cause, too, huh?

REVEREND. Let us name no names.

CAPTAIN. [*Leaving the wheel.*] Rector, you've made quite a speech.

REVEREND. We've tried to make ourselves clear.

CAPTAIN. So I'm a-gonna be hog-tied and thrown in a sack and carted off to a padded cell somewhere?

REVEREND. Such forms of restraint as you are alluding to, sir, need only be imposed if the coarser side of your nature persists in keeping a stranglehold on the finer.

CAPTAIN. [*Advancing slowly.*] Reverend Melton—! [REVEREND *beginning to feel some alarm, rises nervously.*] The coarser side of my nature is just about to get a stranglehold but not on me.

[*He takes several menacing steps toward the* RECTOR, *who backs out of the cabin and down into the living room—the* CAPTAIN *following.*]

REVEREND. Now, now! Mr. Rockley, let us not behave like children.

CAPTAIN. Where are you going, Rector?

REVEREND. I see you're not quite yourself this evening. I think I had better return when your nerves are more settled.

CAPTAIN. My nerves are O.K. How are yours? Here, take off your glasses.—

REVEREND. [*In his excitement of getting out of the* CAPTAIN'S *reach the* REVEREND *strikes his nose with his umbrella.*] I've struck my nose. It's bleeding.

CAPTAIN. That's what you get for sticking it in the wrong place.

REVEREND. A most unfeeling remark and quite uncalled for. [*Seeing the* CAPTAIN *in his path to the front door.*] Is there no other way out?

CAPTAIN. [*Starting after him.*] Yes, on the toe of my boot. [REVEREND *starts Right toward garden.*] Christian retreat, eh? Who's retreating now? You come nosing around here again and I'll marry you off to Emmie, like it or not. [*Chases him out the French doors. To* HADRIAN, *who has been watching from the kitchen corridor.*] You hear the goings-on in here?

HADRIAN. Yeah!

CAPTAIN. I think I'll have a drink.

HADRIAN. Matilda didn't step out for a peep at the show?

CAPTAIN. No, but I'll wager they both of them got an earful, skulking up there in their little rabbit holes. [FLORA *whines and scratches on the front door.*] Listen to that clever dog. Remind me tomorrow to buy her a good big bone. She's scratching at the door. I'll let her in. [*He opens the door and brings Flora in.*]

HADRIAN. Captain! Captain! I think we've found our wooden horse. Here, let me have Flora. [*Sends her off to kitchen.*]

CAPTAIN. What? Wooden horse?

HADRIAN. Sh! Matilda's still up. I see the light under her door.

CAPTAIN. Where's the wooden horse?

HADRIAN. Wait and see! [*He steals quietly upstairs to* MATILDA'S *door. Gets down on his hands and knees and scratches on her door and whines, imitating Flora.*]

MATILDA. [*From inside her room.*] No, Flora. Go back to your basket. No, Flora. It's sleepy time. [HADRIAN *continues the whining, more plaintively than before.* CAPTAIN *shakes with laughter.*] Oh, alright. But only to say good night.

[*As she opens the door* HADRIAN *steps in.* CAPTAIN *goes into cabin.*]

HADRIAN. Only to say good night!

MATILDA. Hadrian! What a silly trick!

HADRIAN. You wouldn't come out. I had to see you.

MATILDA. Hadrian, please go.

HADRIAN. Look, Matilda. I'm leaving tomorrow morning and taking you with me.

MATILDA. [*Stepping out into hall.*] Come out of my bedroom.

HADRIAN. Not until you come inside and talk with me.

EMMIE. [*Comes out of her room and sees* HADRIAN *in* MATILDA's *room.*] What are you doing in there? [*She hurriedly closes the door and locks it; keeping the key.*] There! I've locked him in. [HADRIAN *laughs.*] You won't think it's so funny when you find out what I'm going to do. I'm going to call the police. This is just the evidence we need of your bad character. [*Picks up phone.*] Police! Police! Get me the police!

CAPTAIN. [*Comes out of the cabin.*] What's going on around here? What are you tabby-cats up to?

EMMIE. Never you mind. No help is expected from you.

CAPTAIN. Hadrian! The women are up to something!

EMMIE. [*Phoning.*] Police?

CAPTAIN. Holy God! The she-devil's got the law on us! Come out of there, boy.

EMMIE. Come at once to the Rockley pottery house. I've got a soldier locked in a bedroom.

CAPTAIN. Locked in, locked in, huh?

EMMIE. Yes, come quickly, please. He tried to attack my niece.

CAPTAIN. He didn't try to attack her.

EMMIE. I tell you he did.

CAPTAIN. [*Crosses to* MATILDA'S *door; tries to open it. From the landing.*] Where's the key?

EMMIE. I've got it. I've got it.

CAPTAIN. [*As he comes downstairs.*] You let him out. Do you hear me. You let him out or I'll smash everything in this God-damned house to pieces. Smash it to smithereens!

EMMIE. Go on, do that. That's all the proof we need of your absolute madness.—Go on, smash everything.

CAPTAIN. [*Crosses to* MATILDA.] Matilda! Matilda!

EMMIE. [*Crossing to* CAPTAIN.] Leave her alone! She's dazed, struck senseless! You want to make her hysterical?

CAPTAIN. You're hysterical. [*He starts upstairs.* EMMIE *moves backward to block him.*] You're hysterical. [*They meet at foot of stairs.*] Get out of my way—I'm going to open that door.

EMMIE. [*Blocks stairs.*] Come on, struggle with me. That's what I want you to do.

CAPTAIN. [*Panting hoarsely.*] Emmie, get out of my way.

EMMIE. [*Backing upstairs.*] I won't, I won't, never! What are you going to do? Nothing!! [*She leans jeeringly over the banister.*]

CAPTAIN. Matilda, make your Aunt let him out.

EMMIE. She won't, we stand together. We're here to protect each other. It's time somebody took control around here.

CAPTAIN. You're right about that. But it won't be you.

EMMIE. [*Leaning witch-like over the banisters at the top of the stairs.*] It will, it is, it's me. The house will be mine completely. There will be no more intruders, no more outsiders. I'll have it the way I want it from now on. No one will come in that door—ever!—without my permission!

CAPTAIN. [*Yelling at her from foot of stairs.*] You want to do with my daughter what you did with my wife?

EMMIE. Protect her from you? That's right!

CAPTAIN. Turn her into a lifeless piece of clay!

EMMIE. That's an astounding statement.

CAPTAIN. True! You weaned her from me. Holy, holy, holy! Nothing but helping others in your dear brain. Some people have got that power—of turning life into clay. You're one of that kind, Emmie.

EMMIE. Insane babblings!

CAPTAIN. But others have got a different kind of power. Their touch turns clay into life. Hadrian's one of that kind— [*He is nearly up to her.*]

EMMIE. [*Retreating a step or two upwards.*] The craziest drivel a lunatic ever gave voice to!

CAPTAIN. But now he's back. He's here—-and in spite of your will to prevent, he's going to breathe the breath of life back into this poor clay figure you're making of my daughter. *Hadrian! Hadrian!*

HADRIAN. [*Steps quietly in the front door.*] Did you call me, Father?

EMMIE. How did you?

HADRIAN. Through the window. I shinnied down a pillar of the porch.

CAPTAIN. Did you hear that, Emmie? Now what are you going to do?

EMMIE. [*Furiously.*] Ugh! [*The* CAPTAIN *roars with laughter.*] Don't laugh! Don't grin—you two! His proficiency at porch climbing won't do him any good. Matilda will tell. So will I. You'll grin on the other side of your faces when the police get here.

[*She crosses to the living room, protectively encircling* MATILDA *with her arm. They sit upon the sofa. The* CAPTAIN *and* HADRIAN *sit Right, opposite them on chairs. The two opposing camps, male and female, face each other across the room.*]

CAPTAIN. They've called the police.

HADRIAN. So? [*He fills his pipe.*]

CAPTAIN. They're going to accuse you of trying to rape Matilda.

HADRIAN. [*Grinning.*] You mean Aunt Emmie is?

CAPTAIN. Both of 'em! My daughter has got no mind of her own. You'd better be off. It's hopeless.

HADRIAN. Run away? No. I'll stay.

EMMIE. I will have you court martialed.

[HADRIAN *grins*.]

CAPTAIN. She means it.

EMMIE. You don't know what a situation you're in. I have a good name behind me—a reputation. When I speak out, nobody will doubt me. Matilda will speak out, too.

CAPTAIN. It's true what she says about 'er reputation. Everyone thinks she's a saint.

HADRIAN. Except you and me—and Matilda.

CAPTAIN. Matilda thinks so, too.

HADRIAN. I don't know.

CAPTAIN. Look at her! All done up like an Easter package in pink and blue tissue paper, tied around the middle with a ribbon. What can you expect?

HADRIAN. Still water runs deep.

CAPTAIN. Nope. Emmie's turned her brain into a little flower-pot with petunias in it.

[MATILDA *sobs and covers her face.* EMMIE *embraces her protectively.*]

EMMIE. Pay no attention to them. [*Glaring at* HADRIAN.]

HADRIAN. I hope the police won't keep us waiting long. I'm getting awfully sleepy. [*There is a burst of hysterical cackling from the hen-house.* EMMIE *stiffens, but doesn't rise.*] The fox!

CAPTAIN. Yep, it's him all right. He's at it again. [EMMIE *springs up involuntarily and starts for gun.* HADRIAN *and* CAPTAIN *rise expectantly. She gasps and returns to sofa.*] Ain't you going to take a shot at him, Emmie?

EMMIE. I do not intend to leave Matilda alone in here for one moment.

CAPTAIN. I guess it's just as well. You couldn't hit that fox with a bushel of beans. [*The cackling increases.*] Hah! That old red fox is just as safe as he'd be in his own dining-room. I can see him out there, tucking his bib in his collar and smacking his lips and whetting the carving knife and fork together as he prepares to eat his bellyful of Emmie's chickens. Now he's saying the grace. "Thank God Miss Emmie can't shoot," is what he says. The chickens all say "Amen!" In hopes of partial appeasement. [*He chuckles.*] Now he's gone to work. "Mmmmm!" he says. "Delicious! Breast of milk-fed chicken. I think I'll have another slice of the white—the hell with the dark. Living conditions have certainly improved!" "Yes, indeed," says the chickens, trying to be as agreeable as they can, but shaking in their boots. Now he's finished the first one up and he's contemplating another. "Who's next?" he says. The chickens all glance at each other. "You first, Clarissa." "Oh, no! after you, Annabelle!" "I wouldn't dream of it. I don't deserve the honor!" [*A third outburst of the chickens more violent and prolonged than the previous ones.* EMMIE *tries to resist the torture but finally succumbs. She rises and swiftly crosses to the gun and picks it up and hurries out through the garden doors. As she leaves,* HADRIAN *rises and goes to* MATILDA. *The* CAPTAIN *executes a little dance step and turns his back. As* HADRIAN *starts to take* MATILDA *into his arms —two shots ring out from the direction of the hen-house and* EMMIE *hurries in. At that moment the door-bell rings.*]

CAPTAIN. [*To* HADRIAN.] The Police!

HADRIAN. I'll answer. [*Crosses up to the front door. Opens door.*]

[CAPTAIN *goes to* EMMIE'S *Right, takes gun, puts it against wall Right of spinet.*]

OFFICER. What's been going on 'ere? [*Enters, crosses down to step.*]

[EMMIE *crosses to Left end of spinet.* HADRIAN *closes door.*]

HADRIAN. You'd better ask the ladies.

OFFICER. [*Crosses down to chair above desk.* HADRIAN *follows down to his Right and above.*] Well, Miss?

[MATILDA *rises, crosses up to Left of* OFFICER *on line with him.*]

EMMIE. Matilda! *Tell!*

MATILDA. [*To* OFFICER.] I'm very sorry. I had an unpleasant dream and woke up screaming.

EMMIE. Matilda!

MATILDA. My Aunt thought that something had happened and telephoned the police. But she was mistaken. There was nothing wrong.

[*She walks past the* OFFICER *and starts upstairs. He follows, speaking to her.*]

OFFICER. I see. Well, unpleasant dreams are my special detail, Lady. Call me any time you have one— [*He stamps out disgustedly banging the door.*]

EMMIE. Do you realize what you've done, Matilda? You should have told the constable.

MATILDA. [*Gets her coat from rack and starts out, calling to the* OFFICER.] Wait! Wait!

EMMIE. [*Hurries after her.*] Matilda! Where are you going?

MATILDA. [*From outside the front door.*] I'm going to Miss Tyler's to spend the night. I can't stand it here any longer.

EMMIE. Well, ask the constable to take you. [EMMIE *returns and starts upstairs.*] A very sensible action!

CAPTAIN. Where is Matilda going?

EMMIE. To spend the night with Miss Tyler.

CAPTAIN. Why?

EMMIE. Because of the fox! She won't return till he's gone.

[*Glares at* HADRIAN *and goes upstairs.*]

CAPTAIN. What do you make of that?

HADRIAN. She'll be back.

CAPTAIN. Come on, let's have a drink.

[*They start into the cabin as—the Curtain falls.*]

CURTAIN

ACT THREE

Scene II

"Watchman, What of The Morning?"
HADRIAN *and the* CAPTAIN *have kept a night-long vigil with much talk and a little drink. The* CAPTAIN *is recumbent on the sofa with his coat for a cover.* HADRIAN *is stretched out on the floor, sans coat.*
Faint pearly grey light—daybreak.

CAPTAIN. [*Stirring.*] Watchman! What of the night?

HADRIAN. [*Rises and goes to the French doors.*] It isn't night any more.

CAPTAIN. Then what of the morning?

HADRIAN. The morning is—like your daughter.

CAPTAIN. In what respect is the morning like my daughter?

HADRIAN. [*Coming to him.*] The fog hasn't lifted.

CAPTAIN. [*Yawns, stretches and rises.*] Here—let me take a look. [*Goes to the French doors and peers out. Something catches his attention out in the garden.*] Hey! Come here!

HADRIAN. [*Joins him at the doors.*] Huh?

CAPTAIN. Look!

HADRIAN. At what?

CAPTAIN. Over there!

HADRIAN. I don't see—

CAPTAIN. [*Pointing.*] Nothing?

HADRIAN. No, Sir, not a thing but the foggy dew.

CAPTAIN. Look, over that way, a little bit to the left of the— Look! It moved!

HADRIAN. [*As if wounded.*] Uh huh! [*He draws the doors shut.*]

CAPTAIN. You saw it?

HADRIAN. Yes, sir.

CAPTAIN. What was it?

HADRIAN. [*Closes the drapes on the silver flood.*] Our Matilda!

CAPTAIN. [*Touches* HADRIAN *lightly on the shoulder. Then turns and crosses leisurely to the stairs.*] Now work fast and remember what I told you. The talk is the *touch.* [*He goes quietly upstairs.*]

[HADRIAN *stands undecided in the pale gloom. The watchful, waiting fox-like quality in him stands out sharply as he listens for* MATILDA'S *approach to the house. When he hears it, he backs swiftly and noiselessly into the cabin and leaves the door slightly open.* MATILDA *enters the French doors. She is a wraithlike figure in her white coat or rain cape which is gleaming with dampness. The music and the tinkling is brought up again. Her manner is unusually shy and virginal and she enters the house as if it were a stranger's.* HADRIAN *makes no sound in the cabin but she is aware of his being there as if she could see him and he is just as aware of her and so they remain for several moments, sensing each other's nearness and quivering with it.*

MATILDA *is the first to move. She steals into the living room and stands near the spinet looking at the door of the cabin. She coughs a little or clears her throat. Then* HA-DRIAN *moves. He picks up his packed valise and sticks the penny flute in his pocket. Then he strides boldly out of the cabin and starts across the living room as if he did not see* MATILDA. *She stops him with a sudden breathless call.*]

MATILDA. Hadrian!

HADRIAN. Why—I believe it's Matilda.

MATILDA. You knew it was.

HADRIAN. How did I know it was?

MATILDA. You saw me from the window.

HADRIAN. Was that you?

MATILDA. You knew it.

HADRIAN. I thought it was just a bit of the fog coming in.

MATILDA. Oh, you're—such a fox! [*Her voices drops very low.*] You're such a—fox!

HADRIAN. Are we going to call names? [*His voice is low and shaking as if with fury.*] Go ahead. You start first. I'm a fox, I'm a charity boy. What else, Matilda?

MATILDA. Yes, you are a fox! And that's why I'm so ashamed of myself for feeling—*anything* but—*shame*—and—*humiliation*— Your conceit and presumption and then your daring to offer to give me up and leave for a sum of money.

HADRIAN. I guess I get what you mean about my conceit. But what did you mean about—money?

MATILDA. Aunt Emmie told me.

HADRIAN. Emmie told you what?

MATILDA. That you'd take money and go if given enough.

[*A pause.*]

HADRIAN. You believed her?

MATILDA. Wasn't it true?

HADRIAN. What a fine opinion you have of me!

MATILDA. I don't believe I—*altogether* believed her— [*He grabs up his valise and starts off again.*] *Hadrian!* [*He stops.*] Where are you going?

HADRIAN. I'm going to catch a train.

MATILDA. Without even saying goodbye?

HADRIAN. I said goodbye to the Captain. I'll write Aunt Emmie a bread and butter note.

MATILDA. How about me?

HADRIAN. You, Matilda?—I didn't suppose you wanted to hear from me.

MATILDA. [*Angrily.*] Hadrian, Hadrian, please don't make me cry.

HADRIAN. I make you cry? Over what?

MATILDA. I'm very, very upset and have been all night. [*He fumbles in his pockets.*] What's that?

HADRIAN. [*Gives her his handkerchief.*] Your nose is running.

MATILDA. —Oh!

HADRIAN. Have you caught cold?

MATILDA. Naturally I've caught cold, out walking all night!

HADRIAN. I thought you went to Miss Tyler's.

MATILDA. I didn't go to Miss Tyler's, I just made up that excuse to get out of the house because I couldn't think here without interference. Such awful, fantastic goings on in the house!

HADRIAN. Last night I used every trick I could think of to get to you. I scratched at your door— I whimpered like a puppy— I shinnied down a pillar of the porch—but off you go scared to stay even under the same roof with me. I wanted you badly, Matilda.

MATILDA. But not any more?

HADRIAN. I'm fed up with your namby-pambiness now. [*She hands him the handkerchief.*] Keep it! It's all very well to be soft and gentle and fading away in the distance. But what I want and need is a woman, Matilda.

MATILDA. —Oh.

HADRIAN. Not mist or clouds.

MATILDA. You think I'm mist or clouds?

HADRIAN. I'd say that you have some qualities in common.

MATILDA. That may be so. [*She crosses to the desk and picks up the scrap book of her poems, her back to* HADRIAN.] They say that the earth was—only a cloud of mist—before creation was started.

HADRIAN. I've heard that, too.

MATILDA. Then why be so contemptuous of clouds?

HADRIAN. I'm not, I'm not. I just don't think they're very practical material to work with.

MATILDA. God used them. Didn't He?

HADRIAN. Yes, but the clouds He used were—fiery clouds.

MATILDA. And I'm a cold one, am I?

HADRIAN. Haven't you thought that you might give that impression?

MATILDA. Impressions can be mistaken. I'm more of an earthly creature than—anyone knows.

HADRIAN. Are you, Matilda?

MATILDA. Yes.

HADRIAN. It's hard to believe from your conduct.

MATILDA. [*Turning sharply.*] Conduct, conduct! What does conduct have to do with people or people with conduct?

HADRIAN. I'm sure I don't know, Matilda. But stood in the sun—I doubt you would make a shadow.

MATILDA. Then look, you Doubting Thomas! [*She drops scrap book on desk, crosses and pulls open the window drapes. The silver light casts her shadow toward him along the floor.*] There's my shadow.

HADRIAN. Sure enough. But a very faint one, Matilda.

MATILDA. The sun isn't hardly up yet. Give it time to grow darker.

HADRIAN. Time is something of which there isn't too much. I have to catch a train in—[*Glances at wrist.*]—twenty or twenty-five minutes.

MATILDA. Damn!

HADRIAN. *What?*

MATILDA. Damn, I said! I said, damn!

HADRIAN. [*Raising his brows.*] Why, Matilda!

MATILDA. [*Crosses quickly back to desk and seizes the scrap book which is bound in light blue silk with gold lettering on it. Crossing hesitantly to him.*] Hadrian! I've something to give you.

HADRIAN. What is it?

MATILDA. This book.

HADRIAN. Your book of poems?

MATILDA. I wish you would take it with you. I never could talk, but it can.

HADRIAN. [*Slowly taking it from her.*] Matilda, Matilda—you're such a romantic young lady.

MATILDA. That I seem ridiculous to you?

HADRIAN. No, no, no—but it's *you* that I want, Matilda—not books, not poems!

MATILDA. [*Pause. She half turns away.*]—What's—stopping you, you fool?

[*He stares at her incredulously for a moment. Then flings the book to the floor and seizes her shoulders. Music and tinkling bells. He holds her off and looks at her for a long moment and then he draws her slowly and raptly into his arms. She laughs softly and pulls away.*]

HADRIAN. [*Goes to her awkwardly, like a boy. He touches her shoulder. He says, choked.*] Little girl with broken doll, Matilda! Matilda, Matilda, Matilda! Ring out little bells in heaven, little silver Matilda, little bells! [*He holds her against him, rocking and swaying in tender delight.*]

MATILDA. [*Laughs softly.*] Don't—be crazy!

HADRIAN. Little silver Matilda, little bells, little bells! She's broken her doll. I broke it. She's slipped away and I've caught her—not far off. Little silver Matilda, little bells! [*He stands still and then holds her off. Her head hangs so that her hair sweeps over her face. He tenderly brushes it back.*] Little silver Matilda, where are you hiding?

MATILDA. [*Softly and joyously.*] Nowhere! [*She throws her arms about him and returns his embrace with an equal abandon.*] Not any more!

EMMIE. [*All at once* EMMIE'S *voice calls out above.*] *Phoebe?* Phoebe!

MATILDA. Aunt Emmie is up.

HADRIAN. The enemy's on the alert. The opposition is warned. We'll have to hurry.

MATILDA. Are *we* leaving?

HADRIAN. Yes.

MATILDA. Together?

HADRIAN. Yes.

MATILDA. When?

HADRIAN. Right now!

MATILDA. Things—clothes—

HADRIAN. Put on shoes! We'll run!

MATILDA. Yes—yes—yes! [*She runs up the stairs.*]

HADRIAN. Hurry!

MATILDA. Wait for me! One minute! [*She runs in her room and shuts the door.*]

[HADRIAN *does a little noiseless jig in the hallway. The* CAPTAIN *appears on the landing half in and half out of his clothes, his suspenders and shirt collar loose, carrying a tie.*]

CAPTAIN. [*Excitedly.*] Success?

HADRIAN. [*Whispering.*] The town is ours!

CAPTAIN. Glory be!

EMMIE. [*Calling out above.*] *Cornelius!* What's going on?

HADRIAN. Mum!

CAPTAIN. Mum!

[HADRIAN *slips cautiously out the front door with his suitcase.* EMMIE *appears on the landing, peering suspiciously down. She has been dressing hastily for early Communion. She wears an elegant, rustling lavender taffeta dress, which she is hooking. She regards the old man with sharp distrust and he stands with an air of dejection on the landing.*]

EMMIE. Who were you talking to?

CAPTAIN. [*With spurious tragedy.*] My—last—hope—gone!

EMMIE. Huh! Hadrian?

CAPTAIN. Gone!

EMMIE. [*Can hardly believe this unexpectedly sudden triumph. She rustles quickly downstairs and looks in the cabin door. The indications of a complete departure are slowly and approvingly absorbed. She slams the door shut and triumph is written boldly on her face as she turns back to her brother.*] So he *has* gone, then! And just as before—without a word of goodbye.

CAPTAIN. You drove him away.

EMMIE. Whatever was done, was done in defense of our home. It's Palm Sunday and I'll make no harsh speeches. I'm willing to overlook what is past. *Or try!*

CAPTAIN. Well, Emmie—

EMMIE. Yes?

CAPTAIN. He's gone—shall we have peace between us?

EMMIE. Nobody in the world ever worked for peace more furiously than I. Now I'm sure we shall have it. I must phone Miss Tyler to send Matilda home. Tell Phoebe I'll have coffee before service. I shall go and give my thanks to the Lord. [*She passes back upstairs.*]

PHOEBE. [*Enters from kitchen with tray.*] Oh, Mr. Rockley, it's a 'eart-breakin' sight!

CAPTAIN. What's heart-breaking this morning?

PHOEBE. The chicken-yard— Oh! It looks as if someone 'ad ripped up a feather-bed! 'Ow is it possible one red fox could do it?

CAPTAIN. You ladies are always surprised.

PHOEBE. Ah, oh, the poor 'ens that escaped!

CAPTAIN. Did some escape?

PHOEBE. Yes, but they're 'ardly to be congratulated. Squattin' up stiff in the trees, poor creatures—demented. They don't even look at each other—just stare into space.

CAPTAIN. It isn't the fox, it's the death of the rooster that's got 'em! Would you call a celibate life worth living, Phoebe?

PHOEBE. What's celibate, Mr. Rockley? Something not nice?

CAPTAIN. You wouldn't care for it. Here, fix my tie, you trollop.

PHOEBE. No, no, no you don't!   .

CAPTAIN. Put that coffee tray down.

PHOEBE. It's me only protection.

CAPTAIN. What do you think you need protection from, you graceless heifer?

PHOEBE. Oh, I 'as me points.

CAPTAIN. Anatomically speaking, I guess you have. [*Starts toward her.*]

PHOEBE. [*Dodging.*] Now, Mr. Rockley, it's Sunday!   ⁻

EMMIE. [*Upstairs.*] Cornelius!.

PHOEBE. [*Giggles.*] Shhh! Miss Emmie!

EMMIE. [*Appears on the landing, dressed for church in her elegant taffeta dress, deep lavender, shimmering and rustling. She wears a heavy gold cross and chain with amethyst mountings. Her hat is impressive and adorned with lilacs. She carries an ivory leather prayer book and white gloves. She is really an imposing and handsome figure. Sharply.*] Cornelius! Phoebe, I'm very late. I'll have to gulp my coffee. Bring it right away. [*To* CAPTAIN *after* PHOEBE *has given her a cup of coffee and gone into the kitchen.*] Why this get-up?

CAPTAIN. Look at me. What do you notice?

EMMIE. The usual aroma.

CAPTAIN. My change of character—ain't that apparent to you?

EMMIE. *What* change of character?

CAPTAIN. I received a call from the minister last night.

EMMIE. Yes? I know it. I hope you received him in a—gentlemanly way.

CAPTAIN. Oh, I know how to be the gentleman, Emmie.

EMMIE. Indeed! You seldom make any use of the knowledge. What did you and—Mr. Melton discuss?

CAPTAIN. Two subjects were under discussion.

EMMIE. [*Suspiciously, knowing only one.*] *Two?*

CAPTAIN. One of them—injured me deeply.

EMMIE. Huh!

CAPTAIN. The other was—gratifying.

EMMIE. [*With an obscure, but sudden hope.*] What was—the other?

CAPTAIN. Evidently you know about the first.

EMMIE. Things could not go on as they had been going.

CAPTAIN. How right you are!

EMMIE. Some radical departure had to be made. [*She drinks emphatically.*]

CAPTAIN. As a matter of fact, I—

EMMIE. You what?

CAPTAIN. I surprised the rector by my complete agreement. After all, when I—well—when I heard the second proposal, I was won over to the first one.

EMMIE. [*Sets down the cup and saucer on the table with a loud clink.*] The—uh—second proposal?

CAPTAIN. When I learned his intentions—I understood his concern.

EMMIE. What intentions?

CAPTAIN. [*Quickly and emphatically.*] *Honorable!*

EMMIE. [*Pushing aside both saucer and cup.*] Will you come out and tell me what you're saying?

CAPTAIN. [*Loudly.*] He gave me my choice—-reform, or a Christian retreat!

EMMIE. But you *must* see that—

CAPTAIN. Sure! I could see how embarrassing it would be to the rector—[*He glances at her cautiously and marches to the French doors.*]—having his brother-in-law in the looney-bin!

[*There is a pause. This is a breathless moment for* EMMIE.]

EMMIE. [*Picks up the cup and saucer as though they were sudden proof of life on Mars—shakily.*] Oh, this is—more of your nonsense.

CAPTAIN. [*Emphatically.*] Nope. "Mr. Rockley," he says, "as your sister's next of kin, I ask you for her hand." "What!" I says. I made him repeat it—twice. Then— [*He makes a broad gesture.*] Well! "Take her hand," I says, "take her foot, the whole of her handsome anatomy's yours for the asking."

EMMIE. [*The church bells ring out as* EMMIE *stares at her brother, torn between doubt and belief. The opinion slowly settles on the side of the angels. Not to appear convinced.*] Uh, you're drunk before breakfast. I don't believe one word you are saying about the second proposal.

CAPTAIN. Could hardly believe it myself. Apparently sane

man! Why didn't you let me know how things were going?

EMMIE. Let you know? [*She aimlessly sets the cup down again.*] Why, it was too—*indefinite.*

CAPTAIN. [*Watching her with cautious slyness.*] I never saw such feeling in a lover. Still having a little natural resentment about the first proposal, I made out as if I might —stand in the way.

EMMIE. But you didn't—did you?

CAPTAIN. [*With abrupt magnanimity.*] Well, after all, why should I?

EMMIE. Heavens, it's—service will start and—I—! I'm not quite sure I can sit through the service.

CAPTAIN. Calm yourself, Emmie. You are not Mother Eve, nor is the minister Adam.

MATILDA. [*Steps out on landing, radiant and smiling. Quietly.*] Good morning, Father. [*She slips demurely downstairs before* EMMIE *can comprehend the alteration in her manner and clothing.*]

EMMIE. Matilda! [*At this cry* HADRIAN *appears in the front doorway.*] Hadrian! [*She runs over and clutches* MA- TILDA's *arm.*] What are you thinking of doing.

MATILDA. [*Breaking away.*] I'm not thinking—I'm doing.

EMMIE. What?

MATILDA. Leaving. Going out!

[EMMIE *clutches her arm again.* HADRIAN *advances and snatches* MATILDA *off her feet and starts for door.*]

EMMIE. [*Following up.*] Where are you going?

HADRIAN. [*Calling back.*] Forward!

[*They disappear. The bells of the church begin to toll again.*]

CAPTAIN. [*Leaning on newel post.*] Forward's the way—for an old man's daughter to go.

[*The bells toll slowly and richly.* EMMIE *stands stricken, rooted in the hallway with her gloved hands clasping the religious book to her narrow virginal chest.*]

EMMIE. [*Slowly and vaguely.*] Well—I shall go on to the church—as if nothing had happened. And I may as well take Mr. Melton's chasuble—with me. [*She takes chasuble and stole from table up Left, starts up the stairs and the* CAPTAIN *sweeps the door open with a cavalier gesture as—*

THE CURTAIN FALLS

COCKEYED
William Missouri Downs

Comedy / 3m, 1f / Unit Set

Phil, an average nice guy, is madly in love with the beautiful Sophia. The only problem is that she's unaware of his existence. He tries to introduce himself but she looks right through him. When Phil discovers Sophia has a glass eye, he thinks that might be the problem, but soon realizes that she really can't see him. Perhaps he is caught in a philosophical hyperspace or dualistic reality or perhaps beautiful women are just unaware of nice guys. Armed only with a B.A. in philosophy, Phil sets out to prove his existence and win Sophia's heart. This fast moving farce is the winner of the HotCity Theatre's GreenHouse New Play Festival. The St. Louis Post-Dispatch called Cockeyed a clever romantic comedy, Talkin' Broadway called it "hilarious," while Playback Magazine said that it was "fresh and invigorating."

Winner!
of the HotCity Theatre GreenHouse New Play Festival

"Rocking with laughter...hilarious...polished and engaging work draws heavily on the age-old conventions of farce: improbable situations, exaggerated characters, amazing coincidences, absurd misunderstandings, people hiding in closets and barely missing each other as they run in and out of doors...full of comic momentum as Cockeyed hurtles toward its conclusion."
- Talkin' Broadway

www.ingramcontent.com/pod-product-compliance
Lightning Source LLC
Chambersburg PA
CBHW072149130726
47909CB00004BB/1326